Why Not?

"So, are you coming to the park after rehearsal today?" Bianca asked.

"Yeah, definitely," Larissa said. She turned to me. "What about you, Anna?" she asked.

I paused, biting my lip. This was the first time anyone from drama club had invited me to hang out, and I really wanted to go. But I had an important *Zone* meeting at Brian's house.

"Come on, Anna, it'll be really fun, I promise," Larissa said, staring at me imploringly.

She really wants me there, I realized.

"Yeah, sure," I said with a smile. "I'll come."

I could just hang out in the park for fifteen minutes and be a *little* late to the meeting. Brian, Elizabeth, and Salvador would understand . . . right?

Don't miss any of the books in SWEET VALLEY JUNIOR HIGH, an exciting series from Bantam Books!

Keepin' It Real

Written by
Jamie Suzanne

Created by
FRANCINE PASCAL

BANTAM BOOKS
NEW YORK · TORONTO · LONDON · SYDNEY · AUCKLAND

RL 4, 008-012

KEEPIN' IT REAL

A Bantam Book / April 2000

Sweet Valley Junior High is a trademark of Francine Pascal.
Conceived by Francine Pascal.
Cover photography by Michael Segal.

 Produced by 17th Street Productions,
an Alloy Online, Inc. company.
33 West 17th Street
New York, NY 10011.

ISBN: 0-553-48704-3

Visit us on the Web! www.randomhouse.com/kids

Published simultaneously in the United States and Canada

Bantam Books is an imprint of Random House Children's Books, a
division of Random House, Inc. BANTAM BOOKS and the rooster
colophon are registered trademarks of Random House, Inc. Bantam Books,
1540 Broadway, New York, New York 10036.

PRINTED IN THE UNITED STATES OF AMERICA

OPM   0 9 8 7 6 5 4 3 2 1

To Laurie Wenk

A n n a

"Ugh—what died?" I asked, wrinkling my nose in disgust. I scooted my chair a couple of inches away from my best friend, Salvador del Valle.

"Actually, I think it's still breathing," Salvador responded as he poked at the food on his plate.

"*I* wouldn't touch it," Elizabeth Wakefield said from across the table.

The three of us were having lunch together in the cafeteria on Monday afternoon. Elizabeth had brown-bagged it, and I had decided to play it safe and get one of the SVJH cafeteria's peanut-butter sandwiches. But for some crazy reason Salvador had ordered the special—chicken chow mein.

"Well, here goes," Salvador said cautiously, scooping up a forkful of chicken and slimy-looking vegetables. Elizabeth and I both pretended to hold our breath as he slowly closed his mouth around the fork. Instantly his whole face clenched into an expression of total horror.

"That good?" I teased.

Salvador grabbed a napkin and spat out the chow

1

mein. He quickly pushed his plate away from him.

"Imagine," Salvador said, still grimacing, "licking the gunk-encrusted tire of a garbage truck just back from a run to the dump—"

"Okay, okay," Elizabeth cut him off. "We get the picture. It tastes gross. Really, *really* gross."

I rolled my eyes. Salvador can be pretty annoying sometimes, but I like him anyway. We've been friends forever, so I guess he kind of grew on me over the years. Like fungus.

"That was a great expression you had, though," I said. "I could try to use it in drama club, like if I ever have to pretend that I'm a prisoner of war forced to eat slop."

Elizabeth glanced over at me. "How's that going?" she asked, pushing a few strands of long blond hair out of her face. "Drama club, I mean," she added.

"It's really great," I replied.

I'd always figured that I'd be a terrible actress since I'm pretty shy. I could have pictured Elizabeth in drama club. Every once in a while she and her twin sister, Jessica, switch places. Even though they look exactly alike, they have completely different personalities—so if Elizabeth can convince someone that she's Jessica, she must be able to act. And Salvador's always performing in front of everyone even if he's not really *acting*.

But the last person I thought would ever join drama club was me—until Mrs. Marill, the school psychologist, suggested it. Actually, *suggested* isn't really the right word. She and the rest of the SVJH faculty were worried that I wasn't "grieving properly" or whatever for my brother, Tim. He died over a year ago in a car accident, and I miss him all the time. Mrs. Marill thought that drama club would help me "release all the emotions that were built up inside me." Basically I either had to join the drama club or keep going to regular "sessions" with Mrs. Marill, instead of just seeing her for progress checks every few weeks. She's this really old woman who peers at me like she's trying to read my mind. Yuck. It was an easy choice.

The weird part, though, is that now I'm kind of glad the whole thing happened—because drama club is amazing.

"Are you still doing those weird be-an-animal games?" Salvador asked, narrowing his dark brown eyes as he reached over to grab a handful of my potato chips.

I sighed. Ever since I joined drama club, Salvador hasn't stopped picking on me.

"Ignore him," Elizabeth said. "I bet you're really good, Anna. I love the way you imitate teachers." She started to giggle. "Like when you pretend to be Miss Scarlett."

"Yeah, do it, Anna," Salvador urged, grinning.

I cleared my throat and tightened my mouth,

like I had just eaten paste and my lips were starting to stick together. Then I narrowed my eyes and threw my shoulders back the way Miss Scarlet, our gym teacher, always does.

"Remember, class, wet bathing suits are a breeding ground for a host of nasty bacteria, not to mention body odors—," I began in a high-pitched voice.

Before I could finish, Salvador and Elizabeth both burst out laughing.

"See?" Elizabeth said. "You're awesome!"

I shook my head. "You guys are my friends. It's different acting in front of a bunch of people who aren't in drama club." I paused, biting my lip. "Our parents'-night skits are coming up in a couple of weeks, and I'm *so* nervous." My palms started to sweat just thinking about it. "I mean, the last time I was onstage for a real audience, I played a glazed carrot in our second-grade Thanksgiving pageant."

"I remember that," Salvador said. "You were the most believable glazed carrot there," he added in a mock-serious tone.

I threw a potato chip at him, but he just dodged it and laughed.

Typical Salvador, I thought. One of my favorite things about Salvador is the way he can make a joke out of anything. But drama club was actually important to me.

I just hoped he'd figure that out soon.

Kristin

I can't wait to show her, I thought as I strode down the street on my way home from school on Monday.

I glanced down again at the paper in my hand, and my heart did a little jump when I glimpsed the red mark that had made me so happy.

A+

I must have taken out every book on Joan of Arc in the Sweet Valley community library. I'd had to get my boyfriend, Brian Rainey, to help me carry them all home. I'd hoped for an A. But an A-plus! It was the first time I'd ever gotten that grade, except maybe on a fingerprint painting I made in kindergarten, but I don't think that stuff really counts.

I finally reached my apartment building and hurried inside. "Mom! Are you home?" I called out as I burst in. I rushed to the living room, pausing in the doorway to catch my breath.

My mother was stretched out on the sofa,

flipping through a clothing catalog. She was wearing her gym outfit—black spandex pants with a tight tank top—and her hair was back in a ponytail. My mom used to be a model, and she still works out at least four times a week and eats only superhealthy foods.

People always seem surprised when they find out that *I'm* Margie Seltzer's daughter. I have her clear skin and blue eyes, but I definitely didn't inherit her tall, skinny body. I've always been a little chubby, no matter how many crazy diets my mom's forced me to go on over the years. The thing is, I'm actually okay with that.

Too bad my mom's not.

I cleared my throat, and my mom glanced up and smiled when she saw me, then patted the spot next to her on the sofa.

I hurried over and plopped down, then thrust the social-studies paper out in front of her.

"What's that?" she asked.

I grinned, then pointed to the big A+ at the top of the page. I held my breath as I waited for her reaction: tears of pride. Hugs and kisses. A quick call to Grandma to rave about how I was definitely Ivy League material . . .

"Very nice, dear," my mom said, flashing me a quick smile. "Good work."

I blinked. Maybe she hadn't seen the plus mark?

"But—"

"What do you think of this suit?" she interrupted, handing me the catalog she'd been reading when I walked in. I frowned, glancing down at the picture. A blond, 112-pound model in a hot pink bikini pouted at me from the glossy page.

"So, is it *me?*" my mom asked.

"Uh, it's nice, Mom," I replied, feeling tears sting the back of my eyelids. "But did you see? I got an A-plus. That's like saying I did a more than perfect job on the paper."

My mom gave me another dazzling, toothy smile, and I cringed. I hate when she uses her "professional" grin on me.

"Yes, you showed me," she said. "And I'm very proud of you. But sweetie, you always do well in school."

I *do* work really hard. But I'd still never gotten an A-plus before!

"So what about this one?" she asked, pointing to another picture in the catalog. "Actually, that one could be good for you—black is a very slenderizing color."

"Um, I've got some homework to do," I mumbled, jumping up. I turned away so she wouldn't see the tears filling my eyes, then rushed into my room and shut the door behind me.

Maybe there was a terrible mistake at the hospital

where I was born and my real mother is out there somewhere, I thought as I flopped down on my bed.

I glanced over at my paper again, lying next to me on the bed. All of a sudden I had this scary image. I could picture myself as Joan of Arc, tied to the stake, orange flames billowing up around me. And then my mother was standing there, wearing her black bikini, frowning at me and saying, "Sweetie, that potato sack you're wearing makes you look a little dumpy."

I groaned and buried my face in my pillow.

A n n a

"Listen up, people!" Mr. Dowd shouted above the chatter. "Ten minutes of warm-up exercises before we start working on the skits." He started to pass around a tattered, black top hat. "Each team draws a slip and creates an improvisation based on the characters written down. Help yourself to props if you need any." He pointed across the stage to a large, cardboard carton marked Property of SVJH Drama Club.

It was Monday afternoon, and I was sitting on the edge of the stage with my two skit partners, Toby Meeker and Larissa Harris.

Before I joined drama club, it was always me, Salvador, and Elizabeth—like The Three Musketeers. So it felt a little weird at first to be around all these people I didn't know. But everyone was really outgoing, and Toby and Larissa had been especially nice to me. They're both really cool people and talented actors, so I was psyched when Mr. Dowd made us all a team for the parents'-night skits.

9

Anna

I gazed around the theater, feeling a familiar sense of belonging. I loved everything about this place—the warmth of the spotlights on my face, the clean smell of the wood polish Mr. Stevens, the custodian, uses to buff the stage until it gleams. I even liked the heavy, blue velvet curtain that was so musty, it always made me sneeze when I got too close.

Quentin, one of the other members of the drama club, passed the hat to Toby, and Toby reached into it and pulled out a small piece of paper. He ran his fingers through his tousled, curly brown hair as he read the slip.

"This is great, guys," he told me and Larissa, his gray eyes sparkling.

"What?" Larissa asked impatiently, reaching up to snatch the piece of paper from him. Larissa has these really long, thin arms and legs. She kind of reminds me of a willow tree—tall, slender, and graceful.

Toby held the slip over his head, just beyond Larissa's fingertips. "A frightened princess, a knight in shining armor, and an ugly, mean troll," he read aloud.

"How is this supposed to prepare us for the parents'-night skits?" I asked.

Larissa cocked her head, and the butterfly jewels in her long, light brown hair glinted in the spotlights. "I haven't a clue," she finally answered. Larissa lived in England for a year with her parents, so she has a little bit of an accent. I love the way she says my name.

"Hey, let's scope out the prop box," Toby suggested. Larissa and I followed him backstage. The rest of the kids were already sorting through an assortment of wigs, hats, scarves, masks, and other fun stuff.

"Hey, if you come across a warty witch nose, it's mine," I told Toby and Larissa.

"You *want* to play the troll?" Larissa asked as she twirled a big cowboy hat around in her hand.

"I'm not exactly princess material, like you," I said with a shrug.

Larissa groaned, dropping the hat back into the prop box. "Oh, *please*," she said. "Don't tell me you're another one of those absolutely beautiful girls with zero confidence. Have you looked in a mirror lately?"

I felt my cheeks heat up with a deep blush. *Absolutely beautiful?* Me?

I wasn't sure what to say, but it didn't matter because Larissa was already digging around for more props.

"Your shield and sword, my liege," she said as she handed Toby a cardboard sword and a silver plastic shield.

"Thank you, my lady." Toby bowed and took the props from her. Then he set them aside and bent over the box, pulling out a princess cone hat decorated with gold sequins and a fluttering pink chiffon scarf.

"You'll really look like a fairy-tale princess in this," he told Larissa. He paused, glancing back and forth between us. "Oh, wait—you were serious about being the troll, Anna, right?" he asked. "Because Larissa's right—you'd make a fantastic princess too."

I let out a nervous giggle. "No, I'm serious," I replied. "I like character parts," I added, wiggling my eyebrows.

They both laughed, and I felt this nice, warm feeling inside. I'm not used to being the funny one, but in drama club everyone always seems to laugh at my jokes.

I couldn't find a good warty nose, but I did stumble on a rubber Halloween witch's mask. Too bad it smelled *really* bad.

"You can use the smell for extra motivation," Larissa suggested when I showed her the mask. "You're an angry, rotten-tempered, *bad-smelling* troll who hates everyone—especially young, beautiful princesses."

Larissa was actually right—it helped to really *feel* disgusting. I had no problem slipping into the role of the troll as the three of us improvised a short scene on a drawbridge where Toby rescued Larissa from me.

"Okay, people." Mr. Dowd's voice echoed through the theater after about ten minutes. "That's it for warm-ups. All props should be returned to the prop box before a five-minute break. At the end of the break I want to see teams grouped together with scripts in hand."

Larissa and I stood up, and Toby slipped the shield from his shoulder. "I'll put the props back," he offered.

I handed him the rubber mask, but Larissa plunked the cone hat on his head before he could take it from her.

"Very funny, *Princess*," Toby said. He smiled, then walked across the stage and tossed the props into the box.

"Hey, I'm going to run to the bathroom. Want to come?" Larissa asked.

"Sure," I said.

I followed her out of the theater, and we started to head down the hallway together.

"Why does he have to be *so* cute?" Larissa moaned once we were away from the theater.

"Toby?" I asked, surprised. I knew they were good friends, like me and Salvador. But I hadn't known that Larissa liked Toby as *more* than friends.

13

A while ago I thought that was how I felt about Salvador. Then we tried going out, and it was a complete disaster, especially since he really had a crush on Elizabeth the whole time. We're lucky to still be friends. At least now I know that's all we should be.

Larissa shrugged. "I guess I sort of like him," she admitted.

"Hey, guys! Wait up!"

I turned around and saw Bianca and Skye, two other girls from drama club, striding toward us. Larissa quickly put her finger to her lips, and I nodded, figuring she hadn't said anything to them about Toby. I couldn't believe she'd actually tell *me* something she hadn't told her good friends.

"Heading for the little girls' room?" Bianca asked when she and Skye caught up to us.

"Yeah, I need a touch-up," Larissa replied.

"Me too," Skye agreed.

We reached the bathroom, and once we were inside, they all lined up in front of the sinks, fixing their hair and makeup in the mirrors.

I stood there awkwardly, wondering what I should do. I don't really wear makeup, and there wasn't much I could do with my perfectly straight black hair.

Larissa caught my eye in the mirror and turned to face me. "Do you want to use some?" she asked, holding out a pot of shiny pink lip gloss.

"Oh—um, I don't real—" I stopped, realizing how lame I would look if I said I didn't wear makeup. Bianca's a ninth-grader, but Skye and Larissa are both eighth-graders like me, and *they* used makeup. "Sure, thanks," I said quickly. I stepped closer to the mirror, then took the pot from her and gingerly dipped my index finger into it. The gloss felt satiny smooth. I carefully applied a dab to my lower lip and blended it across the whole lip, then checked the results. The pink shine brightened my whole face. I finished applying it to the rest of my mouth, then returned the lip gloss to Larissa.

"Which skit are you guys performing on parents' night?" Bianca asked as she rebraided her long, red hair.

"Oh, this one where the girl walks in on the husband-and-wife burglar team, then finds out the guy was an old boyfriend from high school who stood her up on prom night," Larissa replied.

Skye laughed. "Sounds like fun," she said, leaning forward to brush her hair over her head. She straightened up and examined the results in the mirror. "So, are you coming to the park after rehearsal today?"

"Yeah, definitely," Larissa said. She turned to me. "What about you, Anna?" she asked.

Anna

I paused, biting my lip. This was the first time anyone from drama club had invited me to hang out, and I really wanted to go. But rehearsal ended at three o'clock, and I was supposed to be at Brian Rainey's house at three-thirty. Brian had called a special meeting to talk about some problems we were having with *Zone,* the 'zine that he, Salvador, Elizabeth, and I work on together.

"Come on, Anna, it'll be really fun, I promise," Larissa said, staring at me imploringly.

She really wants me there, I realized.

"Yeah, sure," I said with a smile. "I'll come."

I could just hang out in the park for fifteen minutes and be a *little* late to the meeting. Brian, Elizabeth, and Salvador would understand . . . right?

How to Turn Fifteen Minutes into Thirty-five Minutes

3:10 P.M. The drama-club group arrives at the park. Larissa buys a pretzel with extra mustard from a vendor. Toby threatens to paint mustard mustaches on Larissa and Anna.

3:13 P.M. Quentin, wearing a crown of dandelions, starts waltzing with Skye, singing "I Feel Pretty," from *West Side Story*, at the top of his lungs. Dan is sprawled on the grass, laughing so hard, he can't stand up.

3:15 P.M. Toby chases after Anna and Larissa, waving a mustard-covered index finger at them. Anna manages to clamber to the top of a jungle gym for safety. Oddly, Larissa isn't running away all that fast.

3:18 P.M. Bianca, taking a yoga break, assumes the lotus position. Quentin, taking a break from singing and dancing, assumes the klutz position beside her. He loses his balance and topples over, knocking Bianca onto the grass.

3:25 P.M.   Toby tackles Larissa and smears some mustard across her cheek. Anna valiantly tries to come to the rescue and ends up with a face covered in mustard for her efforts.

3:27 P.M.   Dan and Skye begin to pantomime a tug-of-war—a favorite drama warm-up exercise. Quentin and Bianca, bored, take sides in the improvisation.

3:32 P.M.   Anna and Larissa team up to get revenge on Toby, smearing mustard across his cheeks. After laughing and pointing at each other for several minutes, they decide to run into a nearby diner and grab some napkins to clean themselves off.

3:42 P.M.   Quentin's team "wins" the tug-of-war. Both teams collapse onto the grass, laughing.

3:45 P.M.   Anna, Larissa, and Toby are on their way back to join the others when Anna glances at her watch and gasps, "The *Zone* meeting!" She takes off, shouting her good-byes as she races across the park.

Elizabeth

I drummed my fingers nervously on Brian Rainey's desk, then glanced over at Salvador. He was sitting on the edge of Brian's bed, fumbling around with an old Rubik's Cube. He'd been playing with it for the last twenty minutes while we all waited for Anna to show up.

"Brian, are you sure you told her the meeting was at your house?" Salvador asked without looking up from the cube.

"Yep," Brian answered.

"Today? At three-thirty?"

"Sal, I told her everything," Brian said, sounding slightly exasperated.

"She probably just got held up in rehearsal," I offered.

Salvador snorted, tossing the Rubik's Cube into a basket of junk next to Brian's bed. He stood up and started pacing across the room. "It's not like Anna to be late," he muttered.

The doorbell rang downstairs, interrupting Salvador's grumbling, and I sighed in relief.

Brian jumped up. "That's probably her," he said, heading out of his bedroom. "I'll be right back."

I heard Brian's footsteps fade as he went downstairs. A minute later he came back up into the room with Anna behind him.

My eyes widened slightly when I caught sight of Anna. The hair framing her face was wet with perspiration, and her cheeks were flushed, like she'd been running. There were also some weird yellow specks right near her nose—I had no clue what they were. It almost looked like *mustard* spots. Her lips seemed to have an extra glow too. I squinted and looked closer, realizing she was wearing lip gloss.

"Sorry I'm late," she said between deep breaths. She glanced back and forth between me and Salvador as she set her backpack down on Brian's bed. "I was just telling Brian I got caught up in the park with—"

"Skip it," Salvador said, a slight edge to his voice. "Let's get this meeting started."

Anna shot me a questioning glance. I gave her a smile to show I wasn't mad, but I had a feeling Salvador wasn't going to let this go.

Brian plopped back down next to me at his desk. "Okay, we've got a lot of stuff to go over," he began. "*Zone's* in big trouble. It's taking us so long to get an issue out that the news is old by the time it's published." He shrugged. "I mean, it's not even *news* anymore. So how can we start getting *Zone* published faster?"

"I've got an idea," Anna said. "Why don't we work on freeing up our creativity? If we're more creative, we'll get more accomplished."

Salvador folded his arms across his chest, narrowing his eyes into a glare.

"What do you mean?" Brian asked, leaning forward.

"Well, we do it all the time in drama." Anna jumped up and began to sway in a graceful, rhythmic dance. "I'm imagining I'm a tree, blowing in a gentle breeze," she whispered in a dreamy voice. She raised her arms in a delicate gesture. "I'm a weeping willow," she said softly. "Come on, try it. It really works."

"I don't think so." Brian shook his head. He shot a glance out his doorway, probably worried his older brother, Billy, would see us and make fun of him.

I had to admit, I really wasn't in the mood to impersonate shrubbery either.

Anna stopped moving, then placed her hands on her hips and frowned. "You guys just aren't open to new things," she said. It sounded like something she'd probably heard from her drama teacher.

"No," Salvador said, his dark eyes glittering angrily. "We're just not open to acting like idiots."

Anna's mouth hung open, and I could tell she was really hurt. "For your information," she said, her voice wavering slightly, "Mr. Dowd says that exercise is very *poetic.*"

"Try psychotic," Salvador countered, stretching his arms out behind him.

I winced. This was getting way too harsh. I knew Salvador was just being a jerk because he was jealous that Anna had something new in her life. But pretty soon he was going to say something he'd really regret.

"Um, let's get back to *Zone,*" I interrupted. "Brian's right. The reviews we did in the last issue were all totally outdated by the time the paper came out. None of the movies were even playing anymore."

Anna plunked back down on the carpet. "Does the *Spec* have this problem too?" she asked.

"No, it's usually pretty current," Brian replied.

"Of course, everyone on the *Spec's* staff manages to get to meetings on time," Salvador snapped.

I shifted uncomfortably in my chair, wishing I were somewhere—anywhere—else.

Anna looked like she wanted to strangle Salvador on the spot. "I already apologized for being late," she responded coldly.

"Hey, no problem, Anna," Salvador said. "I totally understand. It must take a lot of extra time to put all that shiny gunk on your lips."

Anna's face turned bright red. "That shiny gunk happens to be lip gloss, you dumb—"

"Okay, guys," Brian cut in. "It doesn't seem like we're going to get much done today. Why don't we all try to think on our own about what to do, then we can get together again soon and see what everyone's come up with."

"Fine with me," Anna said.

"You think you can manage to make it on time next meeting?" Salvador asked.

"That's *it*," Anna exclaimed. She got up and stormed out of the room. I listened as her footsteps pounded down the stairs.

Salvador stayed where he was for a minute, avoiding my gaze. Then he stood up and walked out after her, staring down at the floor.

I let out my breath, then glanced over at Brian.

He shook his head. "One more meeting like this one," he said softly, "and there won't be a *Zone*."

Salvador

"So how was your meeting?" the Doña asked as I walked into the kitchen on Monday night.

The Doña is the special name I have for my grandmother. My mom and dad are in the military, and they move around a lot, so we all decided it was best for me to live here in Sweet Valley with the Doña. She's an awesome cook and—this may come as a surprise—a really cool person to hang out with. She takes lots of different crazy classes all the time, like fencing and dancing lessons.

I grunted, rubbing my temples as I sank into a chair at the kitchen table. "I don't know what's wrong with Anna lately," I muttered. "But she's really weirding me out."

"Define 'weirding out,'" the Doña said. She was grating fresh ginger for a special vegetarian stir-fry recipe she'd just learned.

"Well, for one thing, she came late to the *Zone* meeting." I grabbed a carrot and started nibbling on it. "You know Anna," I went on. "She's always been superresponsible."

"Did she tell you why she was late?" the Doña asked. She poured a small amount of peanut oil into a heated wok. It sizzled and popped like a hundred minifirecrackers.

"Yeah. She was hanging out with those losers from drama club, and she said she just lost track of time or whatever."

"That sounds reasonable," the Doña said, spooning the vegetables into the wok. The smell of ginger cooking made my mouth water.

Doesn't she get it? I wondered. Usually the Doña understands things better. Didn't she realize that if Anna was doing un-Anna kinds of stuff, it meant she was changing? And *that* could mean she'd want to make new friends?

Maybe even a new best friend, I thought with a shudder.

"Oh, I forgot the really crazy part," I continued. "She was wearing some shiny pink stuff on her lips. *Anna.*"

"You mean lip gloss?" the Doña asked. "That really is crazy." It almost seemed like she was smiling or trying to hide a smile. She thought this was *funny?*

"What's so amusing about lip gloss?" I snapped.

The Doña grinned and reached over to tousle

25

my hair. "Nothing," she replied, still smiling. "Dinner will be ready soon. Go wash your hands."

I gave her a confused glance as I headed out of the kitchen. Now *she* was acting weird too. Was there anyone normal left in my life?

Instant Messages

KGrl99:	Hey, Bri, how was your meeting?
BRainE:	OK, I guess. Well, actually not really OK. Salvador and Anna kinda blew up at each other.
KGrl99:	What??? Why?
BRainE:	The whole thing's really stupid. Anyway, was ur mom totally psyched about the A+++++?
KGrl99:	:) Thanks, Bri . . . It was just one plus.
BRainE:	So? What'd she say?
KGrl99:	I don't know. Um, I've actually gotta go.
BRainE:	R u OK?
KGrl99:	Yeah. My mom needs the phone line.
BRainE:	OK. Call me later.
KGrl99:	Sure. Bye, Brian.

Kristin

"I think that's all we need to discuss today," Ms. Kern announced at the end of the student-government meeting on Tuesday morning. Ms. Kern teaches music, and she's also the SG adviser. "Thanks for coming, everyone," she added as people started to pack up their stuff and head out.

The bell rang, and the room cleared out except for me. I paused, staring down at the desk in front of me.

It's not like last night was the first time my mom ever hurt my feelings, but for some reason I hadn't been able to stop thinking about it all day. I'd been having trouble focusing in my classes, and all I wanted to do now was stay right where I was. Being in the student-government room reminded me that my class had chosen *me* to be eighth-grade president, which always cheered me up.

"Kristin? Are you okay?"

I glanced up and saw Ms. Kern standing in front of me with a worried frown.

I forced a smile. "I'm fine, thanks," I said. "Just tired."

She smiled. "You have a lot on your plate, I know," she told me, shaking her head. "But you're handling it very well. I think you're doing a wonderful job as president."

"Really?" I asked, flattered. Ms. Kern is one of the younger teachers at SVJH—and definitely one of the nicest. When she gives me a compliment, it means a lot because I really respect her.

Ms. Kern nodded. "Yes, definitely," she said, brushing out a wrinkle in her long, flowered skirt.

"Thanks," I said, finally standing up. "I guess I should go. I'll see you later."

I headed out of the room just as the second bell stopped ringing. The hallway was practically deserted.

"Hey, Kristin!"

I turned and saw my friend Jessica Wakefield striding toward me. Her blond ponytail bounced as she walked.

"Hey, Jess," I said. "What's up?"

She shrugged. "The usual," she replied. "Nothing exciting."

I smiled. "Not even with Damon?" I teased. Damon's her gorgeous boyfriend. He's friends with Brian, and he's a really nice guy.

Jessica laughed. "Things are fine with Damon,"

she said as she started to walk down the hall with me. "But I feel like there's nothing new to do, you know? It's always the same old stuff."

We reached Jessica's locker, and I waited while she put away a few books.

"What we really need," Jessica began as she struggled to extricate her history textbook and avoid an avalanche of CDs, scrunchies, smelly gym clothes, and loose-leaf paper, "is some kind of big school activity." She finally got her book out and shoved everything back inside, then slammed the locker door shut and turned to face me. "Something that would bring everyone together," she continued. "Something really fun."

"Like what?" I asked.

Jessica shrugged. "*You're* class president," she pointed out. "Why don't you think of something?" She held up her history textbook. "I have to study for our quiz. I'll see you later."

She jogged off, and I stayed there for a minute, leaning up against the lockers.

Maybe planning a big school activity would be a good idea. It would keep me busy—too busy to think about other stuff.

I could definitely use a distraction, I thought. All I had to do was figure out what that distraction should be.

Elizabeth

"Are you sure you don't see Anna anywhere?" Salvador asked for the fifth time as we stood at the entrance to the cafeteria, searching the room. The lunchroom was mobbed today. Even our usual table was taken.

"Sal, she's not here," I replied, shaking my head. "Maybe she went to the library to study or something. Let's just get a table, and I'll keep a lookout for her while you buy your lunch."

"Okay," Salvador agreed with a frown. "Want anything?"

"No thanks," I said.

I started to weave through the crowd toward an empty table in the back. I was just sitting down when I heard a familiar laugh.

Anna.

I turned around and scanned the area. It took me a minute to find her because she had her long hair up in a maroon velvet scrunchie, and I'd never seen her hair up before.

She was sitting with some of the other kids

from drama club, and it seemed like she was in the middle of a story. Everyone at the table was watching her, and they all seemed pretty into whatever she was saying. She made some big gesture with her hands, and the rest of them burst out laughing.

I couldn't help feeling a small pang. Anna looked like she was having so much fun.

I shook my head. Despite how Salvador obviously felt, Anna could make new friends, and it didn't mean she liked *us* any less.

I began unpacking my lunch, then glanced over at the lunch line. Salvador had just come out with his tray, and he was gazing around the room. I caught his eye, then waved him over. He grinned and headed toward me.

Please don't notice Anna, I thought, even though I knew he would any second now.

Suddenly Salvador's whole body seemed to stiffen, and a scowl came over his face.

I guess he saw her, I thought, wincing.

He stalked over to me and dropped his tray down on the table with a loud bang. He shot a glance in Anna's direction, but she didn't turn around. He frowned, then sat down with his back to her. "I see Princess Ah-na is holding court," he grumbled.

He had started calling her "Ah-na" ever since

she mentioned that one of the girls in drama club has a British accent.

"Salvador," I started cautiously, "it's no big deal if Anna eats lunch with someone else once in a while."

He snorted. "I guess we're just a little too un-sophisticated for her," he said, ignoring my comment. He took a big bite of his cheeseburger and chomped on it loudly.

"So, what's the Doña up to these days?" I asked, trying to sound cheerful. I unpeeled the wrapping from my sandwich, then picked up my juice and took a few sips.

"The usual," Salvador answered, sounding distracted. "Tai chi. Mediterranean cooking. Fencing. Ballroom dancing." He squirted ketchup onto his fries. "Oh, I almost forgot. She joined a senior-citizen cheerleading squad."

I almost choked on my juice. "You're kidding. Who's she cheering for?"

Salvador popped a french fry into his mouth. "A softball team made up of senior citizens. The Silver Streaks."

"No way!" I laughed. "What's her squad called?"

"The Silver Belles." Salvador wiped his mouth with his napkin and twisted around to cast a quick glance at Anna. Then he looked back at me. "Hey, I'll demonstrate one of their routines," he suggested.

"No. Come on, Salvador, not here in the—"

But Salvador was already standing up, his arms stretched out above him.

What was he trying to do? Was he so determined to get a reaction from Anna that he'd risk making fools of us in front of the whole, crowded cafeteria?

Salvador spun around to face Anna's table.

"Give me an *s!*" he shouted in a high-pitched, loud voice. He started waving his arms wildly. Some kids behind me burst out laughing. Anna seemed oblivious.

Lucky Anna.

"Salvador, please!" I pleaded, grabbing hold of his arm. "Sit down! You're acting like a jerk!"

Salvador shrugged out of my grasp, but he stopped his "cheer" and sank back down into his seat.

I started to relax, figuring he'd given up, but then he jumped up again, holding on to a napkin he'd crumpled into a ball.

"So, did anyone see the Lakers game last night?" he bellowed.

Lakers? Salvador *hates* sports!

I stared up at him in confusion and horror.

"They were awesome, right?" he yelled. "They toss the ball in with three seconds left—and *score!* They win with no time left in the game!" He pitched the napkin across the cafeteria. It looked like he was aiming at a garbage can a few feet away from Anna's table.

I knew better.

The napkin sailed through the air, careened off Ronald Rheece's left shoulder, whizzed past Sheila Watson's right ear—and landed right in Charlie Roberts's drink.

Charlie's the editor of the *Zone*'s rival paper, the SVJH *Spectator*. She's the reason we quit the *Spec* and started *Zone* in the first place—she's *not* a nice person, and Salvador and I aren't exactly on her top-ten list of favorite people.

Charlie whipped her head around and surveyed the crowd. Her dark red lips were drawn into a tight, straight line. Soda dripped from her horn-rimmed glasses.

"I think we should get out of here," I said quietly.

Salvador nodded, and I quickly shoved all my food back into the bag, then ran after him toward the exit.

Kristin

Something fun, I mused as I headed toward the music department during my break on Tuesday afternoon. It had stuck in my head ever since I'd talked to Jessica, and I'd finally decided to go see if Ms. Kern had any ideas.

I reached Ms. Kern's classroom, and the door was open, so I walked inside. Ms. Kern was sitting behind her desk, bent over a book.

"Do you have a minute?" I asked from the doorway.

She glanced up and smiled. "Oh, hello, Kristin," she said. "Come on in."

I walked in and sat down in one of the chairs to the left of her desk. "Are you sure it's not a bad time?" I asked, pointing at the book she'd been reading.

Ms. Kern shook her head. "No, of course not," she said. She closed the book and put it aside. "What's on your mind?"

"Well," I began, leaning back in my chair, "my friend and I were talking about planning some kind of big school activity. Something really *fun* where everyone could get into it, like with different games and—" I stopped as something hit me. "Have we ever had a carnival here before?" I asked eagerly.

Ms. Kern cocked her head thoughtfully. "I don't know," she replied. "That's an interesting idea, but we would need to get permission from Principal Todd. And then if he agreed, it would be a huge project. You'd have to budget money for supplies, pull together a committee of volunteers to help set everything up—" She paused, pursing her lips. "You know, Bethel's pretty busy right now with the athletes' brunch coming up, but we could get the presidents and vice presidents from other classes to help. And I'd be happy to put in extra time."

"Really? Wow—thanks," I said, feeling my face light up. Bethel McCoy's the eighth-grade-class vice president. She's on the track team, and so far most of the student-government things she's worked on have been sports stuff. Actually, we haven't really planned anything together as a team—but I don't think that's a bad thing since Bethel and I have never gotten along really well anyway.

"I'll tell you what," Ms. Kern said. "I'll talk to Principal Todd tomorrow morning, and then if he agrees, you and I can meet in the cafeteria at lunch and start organizing things. Does that sound okay?"

"Yeah—definitely," I said. I jumped up, running a hand quickly through my long hair. "Thanks so much, Ms. Kern. I'll see you tomorrow."

I turned and walked out of the room, feeling excited for the first time all day.

A n n a

"This is my stop," Larissa told me as the bus pulled up to the curb.

I grabbed my backpack and followed Larissa off the bus, then walked with her down the street toward her house. It was a big, white house with a really cool design—like something out of an art magazine. It had all these sloping walls and large, glass-paneled windows.

Larissa had invited me and Toby to come over after school and run lines for our skit. Even though Toby said he had to study for a test, Larissa and I had decided we could still work on our parts without him.

"Mum's probably working out back," Larissa said as she slipped her key into the lock on the front door. Her key ring had this pretty marble peace sign hanging from it. "Mum's a sculptor," she explained. "Come on in," she said as the door swung open.

Walking through Larissa's house was like taking a stroll through an art museum. I paused in front of this humongous painting of a woman with a blue face and bright orange hair sprawled on a bright green rug. It was pretty amazing— but I wasn't sure I *got* it exactly.

We passed through the kitchen to the backyard, where a tall, blond woman was up to her elbows in wet clay.

"Mum, this is Anna." Larissa kissed her mother on the cheek, and then her mom turned to flash me a warm smile. "Nice to meet you, Anna," she said.

Larissa nodded at her mother's worktable. "What's that supposed to be?" she asked.

"This," her mother said, frowning at the slimy mound of wet, gray clay, "is supposed to be a sculpture of Mrs. MacMurray, our next-door neighbor." She had a much heavier accent than Larissa did. I guess maybe she lived in England for longer, back before Larissa was born.

"Anna and I are going up to my room to run lines for a while," Larissa said. "Any chips in the kitchen?"

"A whole bag full," her mom replied. "And there's a fresh bowl of salsa in the fridge," she called after us. "Help yourselves, girls."

Minutes later we were sprawled on Larissa's loft bed, munching away.

Larissa's room had so much *stuff*. Her walls were covered with posters of rock groups I'd never even heard of. I guess they were British bands. She'd also hung brightly colored beaded curtains in the windows instead of regular curtains or blinds. It made the windows look like stained glass.

Larissa followed my gaze to the poster with the words *Vauxhall Road* emblazoned across the top. "Don't you love them?" she asked.

"I don't really know them that well," I admitted.

"I'll lend you one of their CDs," Larissa offered. "Ritchie has the most amazing eyes," she added with a sigh, licking some salsa off her thumb. "Toby's eyes are almost exactly the same color."

I looked at the Vauxhall Road poster again, wondering which of the guys was Ritchie.

"So, do you really like Toby a lot?" I asked, nibbling on a chip.

"Yeah, I think so," Larissa said. She smiled and then glanced down at her bed, toying with a loose thread on her Indian-style bedspread. "I even wrote this poem about him where I said his eyes are like 'two liquid lights in the darkness.'"

"Wait, you write poetry?" I asked, sitting forward.

"All the time," she replied. "Why?"

"Well, I do too," I said. "And—I don't know— none of my other friends really do."

"What kinds of stuff do you write about?" Larissa asked.

I paused, watching the colors from the

41

beaded curtains dance on the wall. Most of the poems I'd written in the past year were about losing Tim, but I wasn't sure I knew Larissa well enough to talk about that.

"Just, um, lots of stuff," I said.

Larissa reached over to a shelf by her bed and picked up a book of matches and a stick of incense. She lit the incense stick, gently blew it out, and set it in an incense holder. A spicy, exotic smell filled the air.

"So, do you have a boyfriend?" she asked.

I shook my head. "I went out with this one guy for a little while, but it didn't work out."

"Anyone I know?" she asked, leaning toward me with a curious gleam in her pretty hazel eyes.

I wasn't sure how to answer. I figured if I said, "The guy who acted like a total freak at lunch today doing cheerleading routines and throwing garbage across the cafeteria," it'd be easy.

"Maybe. His name is Salvador del Valle," I replied, trying to ignore the knot forming in my stomach.

Larissa grinned. "Short, curly hair and really dark eyes?"

I nodded. Would Larissa think I was a total loser for dating Salvador?

"He was in one of my classes a couple of years ago," she said. "He's cute—but a little immature."

I relaxed. "Yeah, he can be. Actually, we've

been best friends since we were little. I guess that's one of the reasons the whole dating thing didn't work. We're still friends, though." I paused. "You might want to be careful, you know, with Toby. If you two are good friends . . ."

Larissa winced. "I know—I don't want to mess that up. But he's so cute!" She giggled, and I laughed too. "Hey," she continued, "a few of us are going to a play Saturday night at Sweet Valley High. Toby's sister, Sarah, knows one of the actors, so we got an invite to the cast party afterward. Interested?"

"Sounds great." Usually I rent movies with Elizabeth and Salvador on Saturday nights. But this was a *high-school* cast party. They'd have to understand. And seeing the play could really help me out for drama club too.

"You know," Larissa said as she waved her copy of our script in the air, "we'd better spend some time on our own production."

"Right," I agreed.

I tugged my copy out of my backpack and opened it up to the first page, hoping I'd be able to focus on learning my lines when I had so many other exciting things to think about.

To: ANA3
From: BigS1

Hey, Anna,

I tried calling, but your mom said you're over at that drama-club girl's house. If you can squeeze it in, we're having a *Zone* meeting tomorrow at three-thirty in the computer lab. *Make sure* you let us know if you can't come.

Salvador

Anna

"Did you have a nice time with Larissa?" my mother asked as she poured more gravy over my meat.

"Yeah," I said. "She lives in this really cool place. And her mom's a sculptor."

I took a big bite of the pot roast, savoring the delicious taste in my mouth. I'd forgotten what a great cook my mom could be.

When Tim died, my mom got *really* depressed. She wore this old pink bathrobe all the time, and she didn't leave the house or even talk much to my dad or me. Then when she started to get a little better, she went through this whole phase of worrying like crazy that something would happen to *me*. So we ate only superhealthy food. But lately she'd seemed more relaxed, and she'd started making her old dinners again.

"Larissa's one of the kids in the drama club, right?" my dad asked.

"Uh-huh. Oh, by the way, would it be all

right if I went to a play at Sweet Valley High on Saturday night? Larissa said some kids from drama are going, and there's going to be a cast party afterward." I took a deep breath, hoping my mom wouldn't freak out over my safety or something. "This guy Toby, his parents are driving," I added. Cars made my mom especially nervous after what happened to Tim.

My parents glanced at each other, then Mom shrugged and turned back to me. "I don't see why not," she began, "as long as you remember Saturday-night curfew is eleven o'clock."

"Wow—thanks," I said. "I promise I won't be late."

"We trust you, honey," Dad said. He paused. "I bet you didn't know your father was actually in a movie once," he added.

My jaw dropped. "You never told me about that!"

"Well, when I was a graduate student at NYU, I dated a girl who was a film student, and one of her professors was a Hollywood film director—not a major one, but he had made a couple of B movies."

"B movies?" I asked, frowning in confusion.

Dad chuckled. "B movies were smaller-budget films," he explained. "Not big blockbusters. Anyway, this director needed someone to play a pizza-delivery guy, and I just happened to be on the set that day." He grinned.

"That is so cool!" I said. I never thought of my dad as the kind of guy who would be in a movie or even date a film student.

"So how come you never told me before?" I asked through a mouthful of salad.

My father shrugged. "I'm really only in there for a couple of seconds," he said.

"Still, that's great," I insisted. "Do you have the movie here?"

He hesitated, thinking. "Probably somewhere up in the attic," he said. "We can look for it later if you want."

"Yeah, definitely," I said with a grin.

"I'm sure it will be good for a laugh," my mom teased.

I smiled, wondering which was amazing me more right now—the idea that my dad had been in a movie or the fact that the three of us were actually having a real conversation for the first time in what felt like forever.

Kristin

"We could also have apple bobbing, and I can bring in my old dartboard with the Velcro Ping-Pong balls," Ms. Kern said. She'd just finished listing a bunch of activity ideas in between bites of her tuna-salad sandwich.

"Don't forget one of those ringtoss games," I said. "Those are always fun."

Mr. Todd had told Ms. Kern that we could go ahead and begin planning the carnival, but that he couldn't give us definite approval until we passed the budget and activity list by him. So now we were brainstorming stuff to do.

"We should have some more athletic stuff too," Ms. Kern added.

"Bethel would like that," I said with a smile. I finished off my vanilla yogurt and tossed the empty cup and plastic spoon into my brown paper bag.

Ms. Kern frowned and nodded at my lunch. "Is that all you're having? Yogurt, crackers, and juice?"

I shrugged. It was all my mom had packed for me. Usually I grab some other stuff from the kitchen or buy something else in the lunch line, but I hadn't been that hungry today.

"Kristin," Ms. Kern began, staring at me intently, "you need to eat a healthy lunch to get through the school day. Remember, your body's still growing."

"Yeah, I know—my mom never lets me forget it," I said without thinking.

Her frown deepened. "You look just fine, Kristin, and I hope you're not on one of those crazy fad diets."

"No, don't worry—I eat plenty," I reassured her. I paused. "And most of the time I feel okay about how I look," I continued. "But my mom used to be a model, and sometimes . . . I don't know." I shifted in my seat, feeling strange saying this to my teacher. But Ms. Kern seemed like she actually cared.

"Sometimes you feel like you can't measure up," Ms. Kern finished for me.

I bit my lip, then nodded.

"You know, I've never been exactly skinny either," she said with a smile. Ms. Kern is pretty, but she's a little overweight—more than I am. "And I used to feel pretty sensitive about it," she went on. "But then I realized that so many things matter more than what I weigh. I've managed to have a career that I love, wonderful friends, and a fiancé who couldn't care less about the number on the scale."

I started to blush. "Yeah," I said. "I mean, I have great friends, and then my boyfriend, Bri—um, you know, Brian Rainey? He and I are sort of . . ."

Ms. Kern nodded in understanding.

"And I know all that stuff is more important," I said. "Like the other day, I got an A-plus on my social-studies paper, and I was really excited."

Ms. Kern's face lit up, like the way I'd imagined my mom's would when I told her the news. "Kristin, that's amazing!" she said. "You should be excited."

I grinned, feeling my own face light up. Finally someone got what that grade meant to me!

Ms. Kern glanced at her watch, then started to gather her stuff together. "I have a class in ten minutes," she said, taking a last sip of her iced tea. "But why don't we have a meeting after school today for any students interested in volunteering to help plan the carnival?"

"Sounds great," I agreed.

Ms. Kern stood up and smiled. "Great! We can meet in the student-government room at three o'clock. I'll start asking around to see who wants to help, and you can check with your friends too." She paused. "And remember what I said, okay? You have so many things to be proud of. Don't waste time worrying about something as silly as your weight."

I nodded, and she gave me one last smile, then dashed off to her class.

Something as silly as my weight?

If only my mom could see it that way, I thought.

Salvador

"I don't get it," Brian said, his brow furrowed. "I reminded Anna about the meeting when I bumped into her at her locker this morning."

"Hey, if Ah-na is too busy writing her acceptance speech for the Oscars, let's meet without her," I said. I was getting pretty sick of waiting around for my best friend. It seemed like I'd been doing way too much of that lately.

"All right," Elizabeth agreed reluctantly. She rested her elbows on the desk in front of her. "Brian, what was the idea you wanted to bounce off us?"

Brian leaned forward, obviously excited. "What do you guys think about turning *Zone* into a Web 'zine?" he asked, raising his eyebrows.

I glanced at Elizabeth, expecting to see the same outrage in her blue-green eyes that I felt inside. A Web 'zine? What was the point of that?

But Elizabeth was frowning thoughtfully, like she was actually considering this. "I don't know,

Bri," she said, chewing on her lip. "Won't it be really complicated to set up?"

Brian shrugged. "I've got a handle on the basics, and if we need help, my cousin George is a computer-science major at SVU. He'd pitch in if I asked him to."

Elizabeth wrinkled her nose. "It sounds expensive," she said.

Brian shook his head. "Not really. In fact, it'd be way cheaper than printing the 'zine. All we need to do is register our address, then pay for server space." He leaned down and fished a glossy pamphlet out of his backpack. "It should be easy to get the money by selling advertising space to local shops." He handed Elizabeth the pamphlet. "George even lent me some design software."

I saw Elizabeth's eyes widen as she pored over the pamphlet. Clearly she liked what she saw. She offered it to me, but I waved it away.

"Service space, registering addresses?" I shook my head. "You might as well be speaking Greek."

"Server space," Brian corrected. "Come on, everything's on the Web now. And we wouldn't be competing with the *Spec* anymore because we'd be the only Web 'zine. Think how fast we could get everything out there!"

I happened to like *Zone* just the way it was. Why does everyone think that stuff has to change to be better? But I could tell that Brian saw this Web thing as the answer to our prayers, and even Elizabeth was getting into it. Where was Anna when I needed her?

"Wait," I said as something occurred to me, "how are we going to get my cartoons onto a Web site?" I sat back in my chair, confident that this whole idea would be out the window now.

"No problem," Brian replied. "George can lend me his scanner. I just scan in your artwork and download it from my hard drive onto the Web page." He paused. "George has an animation program too, so he can even make your cartoons move."

Animated cartoons? That *did* sound cool, but I still didn't get why we had to change everything in the first place.

Elizabeth shot me a puzzled glance. "Salvador, why are you so against this? It seems like a really great idea."

"Elizabeth, my dad always says, 'If something isn't broken, then why fix it?' *Zone* isn't broken," I said firmly.

"Well, it's not exactly working all that well either," Elizabeth countered. "This would help us actually get stuff out there quickly—even before the *Spec*," she said, her eyes sparkling with excitement.

"Look, guys," I said, desperate to stall. "Anna's not

here, and we can't make a decision until we know what she thinks." Anna hadn't resigned from the *Zone* staff. She was just MIA. Her vote counted— and I was counting on her voting like me.

Brian nodded. "You're right. We need to get her input. We'll have to wait."

"And if Brian and I still want to make *Zone* a Web 'zine, and you and Anna don't . . ." Elizabeth's voice trailed off. She glanced back and forth between Brian and me.

"I guess we'll just have to see what happens," Brian said with a shrug.

I wasn't about to leave it up to fate. I had to find a way to talk them out of this—with Anna's help.

Well, first I had to find Anna.

Anna

"Look up—I don't want to poke you in the eye," Larissa instructed as she swept the mascara wand over my eyelashes.

"Hey, that tickles!" I giggled, trying to keep my head still. We were standing in front of Larissa's locker on Thursday morning, and I'd agreed to let her put some eye makeup on me. "Shouldn't we be doing this in the bathroom?" I muttered, struggling not to move as some guy squeezed past me to get to his locker.

"The light's better here," Larissa replied. She paused, holding the wand in midair, and studied my eyes as if she were peering at an insect under a microscope. I held my breath, waiting for her verdict. Her brow relaxed, and a smile spread over her face. "There!" she said triumphantly, taking a step back to admire her work. "You look great. See?" She held open her locker so I could check out the results for myself in her mirror.

My eyes locked on my reflection, and a small

smile spread across my face. Along with the mascara Larissa had outlined the rims of my eyes with a dark gray eye pencil. It had a very dramatic effect. I wasn't used to seeing myself like that, and I kind of liked it.

"Hey, isn't that your friend Salvador?" Larissa nodded across the crowded hallway.

I followed her gaze and saw Salvador leaning against the wall, arms folded, giving me his version of a death glare.

Suddenly it hit me—the *Zone* meeting yesterday afternoon. All last night I'd been sure that there was something I'd forgotten to do after school, but I couldn't think of what it was. Now I remembered. Salvador was probably *furious*.

"Yep, that's him." I glanced at my watch. There was still a little time before first period. "I'd better go talk to him," I told Larissa. "Thanks for the makeover—I'll see you later."

"Sure. See ya."

I hurried over to Salvador, preparing for a big lecture.

"Listen, Salvador," I began as soon as I'd reached him. "I'm really sorry about—"

"What did you do to your face?" Salvador blurted out, peering at me closely. His face scrunched up into an expression of disgust.

I gulped, a stab of hurt shooting through me. But I knew he was just trying to get to me, and I couldn't let him.

"I'm wearing makeup, Salvador," I said, trying to keep my voice steady. "Why do you have to be such a jerk lately?"

"*I'm* a jerk? Who blew off a *Zone* meeting yesterday?"

I winced. "I'm sorry," I said. "I know I messed up. I was just running lines with Larissa after rehearsal, and I lost track of time. Sal, this parents'-night skit is *really* important to me."

Salvador's dark eyes burned into mine. "The *meeting* was important, Anna. I needed your help."

I frowned. "What do you mean?"

Salvador glanced around us, like he was about to reveal something top secret.

"What?" I asked impatiently.

"Elizabeth and Brian want to turn *Zone* into a Web 'zine," he announced.

My eyes widened in surprise. That was weird. But actually, it could be kind of cool. I know Brian has a lot of computer skills.

"Okay," I said, nodding. "So why did you need my help?"

Salvador gaped at me in disbelief. "You don't actually think it's a good idea, do you?" he demanded.

Anna

The first bell rang. I took a deep breath, shifting my backpack higher on my shoulder. "I don't know, Salvador. I have to think about it for more than a split second." I paused, remembering the play and the cast party on Saturday night. I hadn't had a chance to tell Salvador or Elizabeth about it yet, and I knew if I waited any longer, Salvador would be pretty mad.

"Hey, there's something else I wanted to tell you," I said as kids started rushing by us to get to class on time. "Don't make a big deal out of this," I pleaded, "but I can't watch a movie with you and Elizabeth on Saturday. I'm going to a play at the high school—"

I stopped in midsentence when I saw the change in Salvador's expression. His eyes were filled with hurt, and his whole face sort of sagged.

"—and you and Elizabeth can come to the cast party afterward," I heard myself say before I could stop and think.

Salvador's face brightened. "A party? You're actually inviting your old friends?"

The second bell rang, and I pressed my lips together anxiously.

"Yeah, definitely. It'll be a lot of fun. Okay, we'd better get to class," I said. "I have to stop in the bathroom—I'll see you later."

I ran off down the hall before he could reply.

What did I just do? I wondered. I had no idea how my "old" friends, as Salvador put it, would get along with my drama-club friends.

I guess I'll find out soon enough.

Kristin

"Thanks for coming, Missy," I called out to Missy Greif as she headed out the door after our meeting.

Missy flashed me one of her wide, hundred-watt smiles, then bounced out of the room. Missy is in the seventh grade class government, and she's really eager about *everything*. So when I mentioned the carnival committee meeting to her during break earlier, she'd immediately agreed to join.

I guess a lot of people were excited about this, I thought as I stared around the room at everyone packing up to leave. I'd been shocked at how many people showed up.

I stuffed my notebook in my backpack, then zipped up the bag.

"I think this could be a lot of fun," Ms. Kern said, coming up behind me.

I turned and gave her a grateful smile. "Thanks to you," I said. "You got so many people to come today."

Ms. Kern shrugged. "Everyone's excited about

having a carnival here at SVJH," she said. "It was a great idea."

I beamed back at her. "Thanks," I said.

"Although, I don't know if we'll be able to take everyone's suggestions," Ms. Kern said, raising her eyebrows.

I giggled. "You mean like that guy's idea to bring over wild animals from the Sweet Valley Zoo?" I asked.

Ms. Kern laughed. "Yeah, and I think we might also have trouble getting the high-wire act past Mr. Todd."

I started to laugh harder, and so did Ms. Kern. Soon we were both collapsed in giggles over the crazy suggestions we'd heard today.

"Kristin."

I stopped laughing and whirled around.

My mom stood in the doorway, her arms folded across her chest. I blinked when I saw her expression—her skin was stretched tightly across her face, and her eyes were narrow and cold.

"Kristin, I've been waiting outside for you," she said. "You told me you'd be in the parking lot at four o' clock."

I glanced up at the clock on the wall and winced. It was 4:15.

"I'm sorry," I said quickly, pulling my backpack over my shoulder.

"Yes, Mrs. Seltzer, I apologize," Ms. Kern put in. "It's my fault—I kept Kristin after the meeting to discuss a few things," she said, giving me a brief wink.

I cleared my throat. "Um, Mom, this is Ms. Kern," I said. "I told you about her last night—she's the student government adviser, and she's helping me out with the school carnival I'm planning."

My mother focused her gaze directly at me, practically *glaring.*

Why is she so upset? I wondered. I mean, I know I was late, but it's not like she was waiting *that* long.

"I'm ready now though," I said, hurrying over to my mom's side. "So, I'll talk to you tomorrow?" I asked Ms. Kern, not quite meeting her eye.

"Sure, Kristin. Thanks for all your help today." She paused and looked at my mom, tilting her head. "You know, your daughter has a real talent for leadership," she said.

My mom moved her head in something that slightly resembled a nod. "Thank you for sharing that about my daughter," she said. The last two words came out kind of weird.

"We should really get home," I told my mom, anxious to be anywhere but here. "I've, uh, got a lot of homework."

With a quick wave to Ms. Kern, I walked out of the room, my mom right behind me. As soon as we were in the hall, I had to quicken my pace to keep up with my mom's long, smooth strides. She didn't look my way once, and the only sound in the empty hallway was the clack of her high heels on the linoleum floor.

I shook my head. I had no idea why seeing me talking to Ms. Kern had upset my mom so much—but I wasn't about to let my mom ruin my good mood.

Instant Messages

KGrl99:	Hey Lacey. Why didn't you come to my carnival meeting?
L88er:	Wait—you didn't actually think I'd show up there, right?
Kgrl99:	I told you that Ms. K asked me to get my friends to come.
L88er:	Wasn't your little friend Jessie there?
Kgrl99:	Her name is JESSICA, Lace. She had track. And Brian was busy.
L88er:	Oh. Sorry. But it went fine, right?
KGrl99:	Yeah, until the end.
L88er:	??
KGrl99:	Long story.
L88er:	Uh oh, my dad's looking for me. I'll talk to u later.

A n n a

"Did you know about this?" I whispered to Larissa, feeling panic rise in my chest.

"No way!" she whispered back.

We both glanced at Toby. He shrugged. "I didn't have a clue," he said.

It was the beginning of rehearsal on Friday afternoon, and Mr. Dowd had just announced that today each group would be performing their skit for the rest of the group to critique. I guess he thought the element of surprise would keep us from getting too nervous.

Yeah, right. The thought of performing our skit in front of everyone when we weren't even ready yet was turning my whole body into Jell-O.

"Okay, Larissa, Anna, and Toby, why don't you three go first?"

Of course. Oh, well, at least we'd get it over with.

I had to will myself to stop trembling as we took our places on the stage. I'd done other skits in front of the drama club before, but none as long or involved as this one. As the house lights dimmed, Mr. Dowd flicked on the stage lights. I felt the warmth of the spotlights on my face, and suddenly—magically—I knew I could do this. It was as if all the hard work of the past couple of weeks instantly fell into place.

"Marvin! What are you doing here?" I exclaimed, my face registering shock.

"Susan? Is that you?" Toby asked.

Then it happened. I wasn't Anna anymore. I was Susan—frustrated, rejected, lonely—face-to-face with the man who had broken my heart so many years before. I reached deep down and pulled up those feelings from months earlier when Brian had blurted out at a *Zone* meeting that Salvador kissed Elizabeth. And when the moment came to confront Larissa's character, Marjorie, I pretended I was speaking to Elizabeth, telling her the way I felt back when I liked Salvador and saw her as the girl who stood between us.

"How could you do this?" I began. "You must have known he belonged to me, Marjorie! After all the years Marvin and I spent together. I . . . don't know . . . what . . . to say—"

My cheeks felt wet, and I suddenly realized tears were streaming down my face. My nose was running, and I probably looked gross, but I didn't even care. I could feel all of Susan's emotions as if they were mine, and I just let everything pour out of me.

As soon as I said my last line, the theater erupted into applause and shouts of congratulations. Larissa rushed over and gave me a warm hug. "You were awesome, Anna!" she whispered in my ear.

"You too," I whispered back. Larissa was an incredible actress—she made everything feel so real.

My heart raced as I stepped toward the footlights, Toby and Larissa on either side of me. I was proud, but I also felt awkward—it was fine to be in front of everyone as Susan, but now it was me again—*Anna.* I couldn't help sighing in relief when the applause died down and Mr. Dowd came over to me.

"Bravo! Anna, you really nailed that one!" He handed me a tissue so I could wipe my nose. Then he turned to the kids still seated in the audience. "Okay, thanks to that beautiful performance from Anna, Larissa, and Toby, you now have a pretty good idea of what to strive for. We'll take a quick break, then watch the rest of the skits."

"Oooo, I'm too upset to go on!" Quentin quipped from the back row, pretending to dry his eyes with the corner of his sleeve.

Mr. Dowd squinted past the spotlights. "I heard that, Mr. Thornton," he countered. "Your team's up next, so you'd better get ready fast."

The house lights went up, and Larissa, Toby, and I returned to our seats to hang out for the five-minute break. "I think I'm going to grab a soda," Toby said, standing up again. "You guys want anything?"

"No thanks," I replied.

"Yeah, get me one too," Larissa said. She started rummaging in her bag for some change.

"Hey, my treat," Toby offered.

Larissa beamed up at him. "Thanks."

As soon as Toby left, Larissa slumped down in her seat. She groaned and rested her head on my shoulder.

I smiled. "His whole face lights up whenever he looks at you," I told her. "I think he's just a little shy."

Larissa ran her fingers through her hair. "Maybe," she murmured.

"Hey," I said, remembering my conversation with Salvador earlier, "I invited Salvador and my friend Elizabeth Wakefield to that cast party tomorrow night. That's okay, right?"

"Yeah, of course," Larissa said. "Just promise to make sure Salvador knows not to do anything too crazy there," she added. "It's a high-school party."

I sank down in my seat, frowning. I had a bad feeling that was a promise I wouldn't be able to keep.

Elizabeth

"Why did you agree to come tonight if you were planning on having a miserable time?" I asked Salvador. The Doña had just dropped us off in front of Sweet Valley High, but Salvador was rooted to his spot on the sidewalk. He'd been grumbling about the party the entire car ride over.

"Well?" I prompted. "Do you have an answer?"

Salvador hunched his shoulders and finally started to walk toward the high school. "You don't understand," he muttered as we got to the front steps.

A bunch of older kids were hanging out on the steps, and a few of them gave me and Salvador funny looks as we passed them.

Even though I wouldn't admit it to Salvador, I felt weird being here too. But Anna had made an effort to include us in something she was doing with her new friends, and I wanted to show her I appreciated it. I just wished we could have come with her, but she came separately because she had tickets to the play earlier.

Salvador and I entered the school lobby and made our way to the cafeteria, where Anna had said the cast party would be. The place looked great—it was decorated with all kinds of funky lights and streamers, and music blared out of speakers set up in the corners.

"Do you see Anna anywhere?" Salvador shouted in my ear.

I scanned the room, then shook my head. A lot of kids were there—obviously plenty of people not in the cast of the play had ended up coming. Most of them looked older, though. I didn't recognize anyone from SVJH.

I pointed to a refreshment table loaded with cans of soda and baskets of snack foods, then raised my eyebrows at Salvador. He grinned and nodded.

"I'll be right back," I told him, then headed over to the table.

"Elizabeth," a familiar voice called out when I was almost there. I turned and sucked in my breath in shock.

It was Anna—but I probably never would have realized that if she wasn't waving at me. She was dressed in a white tank top, a tight-fitting black miniskirt, and black platform shoes.

Her hair was swept up in a messy bun, and her lips were glossy red.

I glanced down at my own sweater and jeans, shifting uncomfortably.

"Elizabeth! I'm so glad you came!" Anna shouted above the music.

I forced the surprise out of my face and flashed her a smile. "You look amazing!" I told her.

She came over and gave me a quick hug. "Thanks," she said. She turned around, and I noticed a whole group of people behind her. "Elizabeth, this is Quentin, Skye, Larissa, Toby, Dan, and Bianca," she said, pointing at them as she said their names. "Everybody, this is my friend Elizabeth." She paused, frowning. "Where's Salvador? Didn't he come with you?"

"Yeah, I'll go get him," I said, my chest tightening. I knew Salvador would *freak* when he saw Anna in those clothes.

"Where are the drinks?" Salvador asked when I found him again.

"I ran into Anna," I explained. "Um, just . . . uh, be prepared, okay? I mean, she doesn't quite look like . . . Anna," I said lamely, unsure what else to say. I took his hand and led him back to where I had left Anna and her friends. As soon as Salvador caught sight of her, he started to grip my hand so tightly, I almost yelped in pain and had to let go.

Anna must not have noticed the horrified expression on Salvador's face because she sped through the introductions and quickly offered to get me and Salvador some sodas—leaving us alone with her friends.

We stood there for a minute without saying anything, and I wondered if I'd ever felt so out of place anywhere. All of Anna's friends were dressed like her—in older clothes like the other high schoolers here were wearing.

"So, Crespin," Salvador finally spoke up, shouting to be heard over the music, "you actually like the whole drama thing?"

"It's *Quentin*," he replied, "and yeah, I do. Have you ever acted before?"

Salvador shook his head, wrinkling his nose as if to show that *he* would never stoop so low.

I bit my lip, hoping Anna would return in time to stop Salvador from saying anything too rude.

"But then again," Salvador said, "I was never too big on playing house when I was little."

Dan frowned. "What does playing house have to do with acting?"

Salvador shrugged. "Anna used to really love make-believe games. You could always find her on the playground, pretending the monkey bars were a castle and she was a princess." He chuckled. "Girls," he added, shaking his head.

I glanced at Dan and Quentin and saw their eyes narrowing in anger.

"What are you trying to say?" Dan challenged.

"Yeah, are you saying that acting is for wusses?" Quentin added.

I felt my palms start to sweat. *Anna, where are you?* I wondered, casting a glance in the direction of the refreshment table. Although maybe it was better that she was missing this.

"Hey, guys, chill," Toby said, stepping forward. He placed his hands on Quentin's and Dan's shoulders. "This is a party. Lighten up, okay?" He flashed me a reassuring smile, and I tried to smile back.

Anna had told me about Toby before and what a nice guy he was. I'd have to remember to tell her later that I agreed.

The music suddenly got much softer as a slow song came on, and right then Anna finally came back. She handed me and Salvador each a can of soda.

"So, are you having a good time?" she chirped, looking at each of us expectantly.

Salvador scowled, then popped open his can and took a swig without answering Anna.

Anna's smile faded. She glanced at me, and I lifted my shoulders in a small shrug.

"Well, at least we can hear each other now," I

said, trying to sound enthusiastic. I turned to Larissa, who, along with Bianca and Skye, had been quiet the whole time Salvador was picking fights with the guys. "Your earrings are really cool, by the way," I told her. She had, like, six piercings going up her left earlobe and different funky earrings in each hole.

Larissa smiled. "Thanks. I got it done while I lived in London. Piercing is really big over there."

"I'd be scared to get so many holes," I admitted. "Didn't it hurt to get the ones higher on your ear?"

Larissa shrugged. "Not too much. But," she added as her eyes swept over my outfit, "piercings aren't for everyone."

I felt my cheeks grow warm. "Uh, no, I—I guess not," I stammered.

"Hey, did the guy who played Rusty keep messing up his lines, or was that stutter on purpose?" Anna cut in. I shot her a grateful glance.

"I—I—I'm not s-s-sure," Quentin quipped.

"You thould really do thomthing about that thpeech impediment," Salvador lisped.

Quentin turned his back on Salvador. "How about the girl who played Rusty's mother? No way she's in high school," he continued.

"My sister said she was left back a year," Toby explained.

They all joined in, getting into a heated

debate over their opinions on the play that Salvador and I hadn't seen. Even Anna seemed to forget we were there as she launched into her own commentary on the various actors.

Salvador and I exchanged glances. What were we doing here anyway?

"Hey, Liz. I want to show you something in the, uh, lobby," Salvador said. He grabbed my arm and started to lead me away.

"Shouldn't we say good-bye?" I whispered to Salvador. I glanced over my shoulder at Anna, but she was so wrapped up in whatever she was saying that she didn't even seem to notice we were leaving. I didn't want to interrupt her just to announce we were going. It would probably embarrass her in front of her friends, and Salvador had done a good enough job of that already.

We left the cafeteria just as a fast song came back on. The thumping bass followed us down the hallway.

"Well? Are you ready to split?" Salvador asked when we reached the lobby.

"Yeah, I guess," I said, still worried about leaving Anna like that.

She'll probably be relieved, I thought. She obviously wanted to hang out with her other friends, not us.

Entry in Anna's Journal, Late Saturday Night

Dear Diary,

Sometimes I wonder if who you are has a lot to do with who other people think you are. Like, I've always had this reputation as being a shy, quiet girl, so that's pretty much what I thought too. I wasn't the "type" of person to be into drama or to have a lot of fun at a high-school cast party. At least, I figured I wasn't — since everyone else seemed to think so.

I guess that's what's so cool about meeting new people. It's not just about being surprised by them — it's about being surprised by yourself.

Kristin

It hit me the moment I managed to pry my eyes open on Sunday morning—the smell of something cooking.

I glanced at my alarm clock and shot out of bed. I was supposed to meet my best friend, Lacey Frells, at the mall at ten-thirty. It was already nine-fifteen.

But what's that smell? I wondered as I hurried to get dressed. My mom doesn't *cook*—she lives on salad, grapefruit, and more salad. Whatever it was, it didn't smell *good.*

The mystery was solved as soon as I finished getting ready and entered the kitchen.

My mother beamed at me as I sat down in front of a plate loaded with slightly burnt oatmeal pancakes dripping with gooey low-fat syrup. Next to my plate was an equally appealing bowl of grapefruit sections.

"I thought we might have a nice chat over breakfast this morning," my mom announced brightly.

I struggled not to wrinkle my nose in disgust at the aroma rising off my plate. Mom sat down opposite me and started to eat her grapefruit.

"Well, dig in," she encouraged, waving her spoon at my food.

I prodded the pancakes with my fork. They bounced back like foam rubber.

"So, you're meeting Lacey at the mall this morning?" Mom asked.

"Yeah," I said. "Lacey wants to buy this really cool black dress that she saw last weekend at Fashion Train. And I spotted an awesome pair of white flared jeans in the window."

"Don't get white, dear," my mother said hastily. "They'll make you look . . ." She paused. "Well, you know, white gets so dirty. Pick a darker color instead."

I winced. I knew what she'd meant to say—white makes me look fat.

I squirmed uncomfortably in my chair and nibbled on a forkful of pancakes.

"Is that other friend of yours coming along too?" she asked. "You know, Jennifer?"

I frowned. "Jennifer?" I repeated, confused.

"Yes, the girl with the identical twin."

"Oh, you mean Jessica," I said. "Jessica and Lacey hate each other. No way could I get those two to go shopping together." I'd actually tried it before, and it had been a disaster.

Mom shrugged. "That's a shame," she murmured. She sipped her tea. Every little sound—the clinking of my mother's mug as she set it on the table, the sound of my fork sawing through the pancakes—seemed to be magnified a hundred times in contrast to our awkward silence.

"How's school?" Mom finally asked. I guess she had completely exhausted my social life—what she knew of it anyway. I'd given up telling her about my friends because she never seemed all that interested.

"Great," I replied. I wasn't going to bother mentioning the A-plus again. She hadn't cared the first time she heard about it.

"That's nice."

Another excruciating pause.

My mother's face brightened. "What's that kooky art teacher of yours up to these days—you know, Mr. Drexler?" she asked.

"He was my art teacher last year," I replied, not even trying to conceal my annoyance. "Mom, I've really got to run," I said, forcing myself to take one last bite of pancake before getting up from the table. "Lacey hates it when I'm late."

"All right, dear. Have a nice time," my mother

said quietly. I noticed a sad smile on her face, and I felt a twinge of guilt.

Why should I feel bad? I realized as I left the room and headed for my bedroom. For some weird reason my mom had suddenly decided to act like she was interested in my life. But what was I supposed to do when she didn't even know anything about me in the first place?

At least I have plans with Lacey, I thought. Right now all I wanted was to be as far away from my mom as possible.

Salvador

I settled into the sofa on Sunday morning and grabbed the remote from the coffee table to click on the TV and search for a good movie on cable.

I usually love Sunday mornings. I wake up late, wolf down a stack of the Doña's pancakes, then kick back in front of the tube.

But this Sunday morning was different. It was the Sunday morning after the Saturday night I got blown off by my best friend. I still woke up late and had pancakes, and here I was in front of the TV, but everything felt different. Just wrong somehow.

The Doña was busy in the kitchen, whipping up a batch of baklava for her Mediterranean cooking class on Monday. Usually I'd be in there, hounding her to make sure she saved me some of the sticky, sweet pastry treats, but I just didn't have the motivation.

I was still flipping between channels when the phone rang.

Anna, I thought. It had to be—she was calling to apologize and beg my forgiveness. I was on my feet and halfway to the phone by the second ring.

I grabbed the receiver, then took a deep breath. "Hello?" I answered, prepared to really make her grovel before I gave in. "Uh, no thanks. We're not interested in aluminum siding."

I hung up, my heart sinking. What was Anna waiting for? It was already almost noon.

Maybe she dropped by Elizabeth's to apologize in person, and she's on her way over here now, I thought. The idea brightened me enough to send me into the kitchen to steal a hunk of baklava from the Doña's cooling rack.

"Are you okay?" the Doña asked when I walked in. She shot me a worried glance, her brow furrowed in grandmotherly concern.

"Yeah, I'm fine," I replied, sitting down at the kitchen table with my piece of baklava. "Why?"

The Doña shrugged. "You just seemed a little quiet this morning," she said, closing the oven door. "Why don't you call Anna and see if she wants to do something?"

My body stiffened. "I don't think so," I said, licking honey off my fingers.

"Did you and Anna have a fight?" the Doña persisted. She took off her oven mitts and sat down beside me at the kitchen table.

I slumped and rested my chin on my hand. "Ever since Anna joined drama club, she's just *different*," I muttered.

The Doña tousled my hair. "Salvador, Anna is just growing up. Part of growing up is trying out new things. She has to find out who she can be before she figures out who she really is."

"Well, what she can be is a real pain." I groaned. "You should have seen her at the cast party last night—with her new friends. She was wearing all this makeup, and her clothes . . ." I threw up my hands in exasperation.

The Doña smiled. "It's all right, Salvador," she said gently. "You and Anna can still be friends even if she wears pretty clothes and makeup— and makes new friends." She pointed at the kitchen window. "Remember that dingy, gingham curtain we had before we painted the kitchen?"

"Yeah," I said, nibbling at the baklava. It was still pretty hot, and I burned the tip of my tongue.

"The window looks really different now after a fresh coat of paint and a new lace curtain, right?"

"Uh-huh," I said. "Look, if this little chat about interior decorating is supposed to cheer me up, it's not working. Could we switch to movies?"

The Doña held up her hand. "Just listen," she instructed. "That window still squeaks when you open it, and the top pane is still cracked."

I smiled. "Are you saying that even with makeup and nice clothes, Anna is still squeaky and cracked?"

The Doña laughed. "You're a bright boy. Think about what I've just said." She stood up and headed for the oven. "I think my last batch of baklava is just about ready."

I went back into the living room and started channel surfing again, finally stopping at *Ace Ventura: Pet Detective*—one of my favorites.

One of my and Anna's favorites, I thought with a pang. Of course, now if we watched it together, she'd probably just sit there and insult the acting or something.

I sighed, forcing myself to block out my thoughts. All I could do was just watch the movie and hope Anna was on her way over.

Anna

"What do you think of this for Marjorie?" Larissa held an animal-print bodysuit up against herself.

"Perfect if you were playing a *real* cat burglar," I replied.

Larissa groaned. She held the bodysuit at arm's length and looked it over. "Guess I'd better stick with the black turtleneck and matching leggings," she decided.

I nodded. "Good idea."

Larissa surveyed the store. "How about you, Anna? What are you—or should I say, Susan—going to wear?" she asked.

"How about this?" I grabbed a forties-style black hat draped with dark veiling that totally covered my face and placed it on my head. "Do I look like the dumped girlfriend hiding her pain from the world?"

Larissa snorted. "You look more like a demented beekeeper," she joked.

I frowned and put the hat back but couldn't help giggling at the image.

Anna

"Guess Retro Look was a total bust," Larissa said as we left the store. "Maybe Fashion Train will have some cool outfits for the skit. By the way," she added, "it was really cool the way you got Toby and me together at the party last night."

I smiled. I had sent Toby over to the refreshment table to get me a soda right when Larissa was standing there by herself and a slow song just happened to be coming on.

"If I were you, Larissa, I'd rethink the whole Toby thing," I told her, shaking my head. "He is totally clueless. It's obvious you guys both like each other, so why won't he just ask you out?"

Larissa shrugged. "That's how I like 'em," she joked, "cute and dumb."

I started to laugh, then glanced into I Scream as we passed by, and my laughter faded instantly. Elizabeth was sitting at one of the tables by herself, probably waiting for someone. Maybe Salvador.

Normally I'd run in to say hello. But after last night, that was the last thing I wanted to do. I couldn't believe the way she and Salvador had just ditched me without even saying good-bye. I could maybe expect that from Salvador after the way he'd been acting lately, but Elizabeth? She was usually much more thoughtful. Were they both so immature that they really couldn't handle hanging out with new people?

Just then I saw Elizabeth's sister, Jessica, and their older brother, Steven, walking toward Elizabeth's table. Steven was carrying a tray with three sundaes on it.

I felt a sharp pang as Steven set the sundaes down in front of them. Even now, over a year after Tim died, it was still hard for me to watch big brothers with their younger sisters.

Tim would be able to help me with all this stuff going on, I thought. He'd say something that would make me feel better about what happened at the cast party. Or he'd just tickle me until I couldn't be sad anymore.

I was a million miles away when Larissa's voice broke into my thoughts.

"Earth to Anna, this is mission control. Do you copy?"

I turned my gaze back to her and forced a smile. "Sorry. I just zoned out for a second."

Larissa tugged on my arm. "You've got to see this." She dragged me over to the window of Cut It Out!, the mall's hair salon, and pointed at a mannequin wearing a wig with bright red hair. "Don't you just love it?" she asked excitedly.

"Uh, well, it's . . . red," I said.

Larissa held a few strands of her hair up and inspected them. "I'm tired of boring, predictable brown," she complained.

"Wait a minute, Larissa, you're not thinking . . ."

"Why not?" she asked, flashing me a wide grin. "Red says wild, free, daring—"

"Larissa, if you do this—"

"We," Larissa corrected me. "If *we* do this."

I backed up a step. "We, as in you and me? No way." I shook my head.

Larissa pouted and tugged on my sleeve. "Why not? We'll get the temporary stuff. You can dye yours back to black if you really, really hate it." She reached out and ran her fingers through my hair. "With your long hair you'd look amazing. Come on, it'd be so much fun to do this together."

I glanced back at the wig. It was an awesome color, I guess, just not something I felt like I could get away with. I chewed on my bottom lip as I tried to decide what to do.

Salvador would never believe I'd dye my hair, I couldn't help thinking. *Yeah, and he also didn't think I'd be into acting,* I realized.

"Let's do it," I said, feeling a thrill of excitement.

Salvador

This is serious déjà vu, I thought, shaking my head. It was Sunday afternoon, and I was once again hanging out in Brian's room with Brian and Elizabeth, waiting for Anna. Elizabeth sat on the floor, biting her nails. Brian was slowly spinning in his desk chair.

"I left a message on her machine before I came over, reminding her about the meeting," I said. "I don't know where she is on a *Sunday,* though."

Elizabeth sighed. "She was probably out with her parents, Salvador."

"Yeah, right," I snapped. "She's hanging with her cool new friends. You know, the ones she obviously prefers to you and me—judging from the way she dropped us at the party last night."

"Actually," Elizabeth said softly, "*we're* the ones who left."

Brian leaned forward, his arms resting on his knees. "Guys, we've got to make some decisions about *Zone*—with or without Anna. I want her to be a part of it, but she's just not around anymore.

We can't wait forever. So, paper or cyberspace?"

Elizabeth glanced at me, and I could recognize the guilt in her pretty blue-green eyes. "Cyberspace," she said quietly.

Brian nodded. "Yeah, you know that's what I want too." He turned to me. "Sal?"

Okay, this is where Anna comes in and saves the day, right? I thought desperately, listening for the doorbell. *Like a knight in shining armor. Except she's a girl wearing flared jeans and platforms, and she's not riding a horse.* Who was I kidding? Anna had moved on. *Zone* was part of her past.

Worst of all, so was I.

I shrugged. "Fine," I muttered. "Put it on the Web—I don't care."

Brian grinned. "I know you don't believe me now," he said. "But trust me, you'll be psyched when you see what we can do. You won't regret this, I promise."

I already did.

I picked up a copy of *Zone* from the floor and flipped through the pages. *Good-bye, Zone,* I thought.

Brian spun around to face his computer and started frantically typing away.

Elizabeth got up and stood behind Brian, watching what he was doing. She glanced back at me over her shoulder. "Salvador, aren't you going to help?"

I stretched out on the bed and folded my arms beneath my head. "Whatever you guys decide will be fine with me."

Elizabeth cocked her head. "Are you sure?" she asked.

I smiled. "Maybe I'll jump in when you've just about got it all set up and mess everything up by pounding on the keys," I joked.

"Don't even think about it," Brian muttered, his eyes glued to the screen. "Yes! We're registered!"

"What's next?" Elizabeth asked.

"I'll need to launch the design program." Brian clicked the mouse, and images flashed across the screen. "The header of the 'zine is printed in dark blue now," he explained. "But we can change the color of the type to just about any shade you can imagine."

"How about dark green?" Elizabeth suggested. "Salvador, what do you think of this color?" She waved me over to check it out.

I got the feeling Elizabeth was determined to pull me into the process whether I liked it or not. Reluctantly I got up and joined her beside Brian. "Great," I said, barely looking at the dark green box on the screen.

What did it matter anyway? What really mattered was that Anna should have been there. And she wasn't.

VIBRANCE! Hair-Colour
Instructions

1. Drape enclosed plastic wrap over your clothes. *VIBRANCE! Hair Colour* will leave permanent stains on exposed material.

2. Massage enclosed *VIBRANCE! Hair Colour* into hair from roots to ends. Wrap a towel around your hair, and let it sit for approximately twenty minutes if your hair is above your shoulders, thirty minutes if your hair is below your shoulders.

3. Rinse hair with enclosed shampoo packet. Follow up with conditioner if desired.

4. Dry hair.

5. Show off your new color to everyone you know!

Anna

I stood outside my house on Sunday afternoon, too nervous to open the door. For a split second I actually considered pulling up the hood of my jacket to hide my hair.

Relax, I told myself. My parents would get over this. Somehow.

Larissa and I had stopped by her house after the mall to use the dye and her parents were totally cool with the whole thing. Then her mom had dropped me off back home.

I took a deep breath, then walked into my house. I could hear my mother and father in the kitchen.

I might as well get this over with, I told myself. I headed straight for the kitchen. As soon as I entered the room, my parents looked up at me—and everything stopped.

I mean, stopped, like in one of those episodes from an old TV show where time suddenly stands still and everything is shown in freeze-frame—except the main character, who in this case would be me, of course.

"Oh my God," my mother finally murmured. She stood motionless, her hands paralyzed in the bowl of chopped meat she had been kneading.

"Well, what do you think?" I asked nervously, running my fingers through my hair.

"Does it wash out?" my mother asked.

My father just gaped at me.

"Dad?" I prompted.

"Well, it's certainly . . . red. That is what you wanted it to look like, isn't it?" he babbled. "Red, I mean."

"*Candied Apple*, to be precise," I said, trying to keep my voice from shaking. "Uh, that's the name of the shade. It's, um, a temporary shade."

Suddenly my father started chuckling. A low, throaty chuckle. Then Mom joined in.

Wait—they were *laughing*?

"Anna, whatever possessed you to dye your hair red?" My mother gasped, trying to catch her breath.

"I don't know," I replied, afraid that any second they would stop laughing and blow up at me. "Um, I mean, well, Larissa and I thought it would be fun to do it together," I said.

"So there will be someone else at school walking around with that color hair?" Dad asked in disbelief, wiping his eyes.

"Well, yeah." I bent down and checked out my reflection in the chrome toaster.

My mother shook her head and started kneading the chopped meat again. "Do you remember when Tim grew part of his hair into a long ponytail and dyed it green?" she asked me, smiling. "You were probably about six or seven at the time."

Suddenly the memory came back to me. How could I ever forget Tim wearing a long, bright green braid down the middle of his back? After a couple of months he got sick of it and cut it off. I think he gave the braid to me, but I lost it.

So that's why they weren't upset—they'd already been through this with my brother. *Thanks, Tim,* I thought. And it didn't even make me sad either.

"Well, *green* hair is really weird," I argued, finally starting to smile.

"Oh, and bright red hair isn't?" my dad noted, shaking his head. "You know, there's just one thing that worries me."

Mom and I exchanged glances.

"What's that?" I asked him.

"Well," my father said solemnly, "I think I'm starting to like it." He began to laugh again. I couldn't help but giggle too.

"Oh, I almost forgot," my mom said. "Salvador left a message earlier. Something about a *Zone* meeting."

I winced. I'd gotten so caught up in dyeing my hair that I'd completely forgotten about the

Anna

Zone meeting—again! They were probably pretty mad. But still, couldn't Salvador have called to apologize for last night instead of just bugging me about the stupid meeting?

"I'll see him at school tomorrow," I said with a shrug. "If you need me, I'll be in my room, studying my lines."

"We'll let you know when dinner's ready," Mom called after me.

On my way to my room I paused in front of the hall mirror and piled my hair on top of my head, admiring the way the light glinted off the red strands.

I liked the new me. And if Salvador didn't— that was his problem.

Salvador

"Did you talk to Anna last night?" Elizabeth asked. It was Monday morning, and the hallway was jammed with kids rushing to get to their lockers before first period.

I shook my head. "Nope. She never called me back. Obviously she really doesn't care about *Zone* anymore."

Or us, I added silently.

Suddenly I spotted a girl with waist-length, flaming red hair, leaning over the water fountain across the hall. What kind of hair color was that?

I nudged Elizabeth. "Check it out," I said, pointing at the girl as she finished drinking and started to turn around. "Isn't that color awf—"

Anna? I sucked in my breath. *Anna* dyed her hair bright red?

I caught her eye, and we stared at each other for a second. I didn't even try to hide my disbelief. She pressed her lips together, then headed over to me and Elizabeth, a concerned crease forming between her eyebrows.

"Anna—your hair!" Elizabeth blurted out. "I mean, it looks . . . really cool."

It was hard to tell from the tone of her voice if she meant it or not.

But I knew exactly how I felt, and I wasn't about to keep it to myself. "Did you have a little problem with the ketchup bottle at dinner last night?" I asked.

Anna shot me an icy glance and turned to Elizabeth. "I needed a change," she explained. "At first I had to get used to it. But now I really like it."

"It's a little . . . bright, don't you think?" I said, squinting. "I mean, a pair of Ray-Ban sunglasses would really come in handy right about now."

"C'mon, Salvador. Quit it," Elizabeth said. "Anna looks awesome. If anyone can pull it off, she can."

"Thanks, Liz," Anna said, with a small smile.

"What's the name of that shade anyway?" I asked. "Fire-eater Red? Lava Glow?"

Anna ignored me, keeping her gaze fixed on Elizabeth. "I've got to study for our algebra quiz. I'll see you later, *Elizabeth*," she said pointedly. Then she turned and strode down the hall toward the library.

Elizabeth immediately shot me a glare. "Salvador, why did you have to be so cold to her?" she asked.

"Me? Cold? Ah-na's the ice queen," I argued.

"I guess this means you're okay with what happened at the cast party Saturday night? And the *Zone* meeting last night?"

Elizabeth shrugged. "I'm not saying Anna's been a great friend lately, but all you're doing is making things even worse." She spun around and stalked away.

I cringed. Soon I wouldn't have a single friend left.

Kristin

"This definitely makes brainstorming easier," I said, licking some hot fudge off my plastic spoon.

"Yeah—now I know we need to have ice cream at the carnival," a girl in the back of the room piped up.

It was Monday afternoon, and Ms. Kern had brought ice cream sundae ingredients to our carnival committee meeting. We'd all made giant sundaes for ourselves while we tried to come up with some more activities and decorations to add to the list we were giving Mr. Todd.

I looked up at the clock, making sure I still had time before I had to go outside. I did *not* want my mom storming in here again and embarrassing me.

I've still got ten minutes, I reassured myself, returning my attention to the melting remains of my sundae. My mom hadn't sounded too happy when I called to let her know I was staying late for the meeting, but she'd agreed to pick me up at four o' clock.

"Actually, Melanie, that's a good point," Ms. Kern

stated. "We do need to include snacks on our list."

"Well," I began, "since it's a carnival, we should probably have—" I stopped as the door burst open. Every head in the room seemed to turn at once and focus on the doorway.

When I saw who was standing there, a huge knot formed in my stomach.

What was my *mom* doing here? I wasn't even late this time!

"Excuse me," she said, her voice tight. Her gaze swept the room, and I cringed when her eyes landed on the bowl of ice cream in front of me. "I'm sorry to interrupt this . . . meeting?" she said, sounding like she didn't quite believe it was possible for us to be in a meeting if we were eating ice cream. "But I have to pick up my daughter."

I bit my lip so hard it started to bleed. How could she do this to me?

"Oh, that's no problem," Ms. Kern said. "We're almost finished here, and I can fill Kristin in tomorrow on whatever she misses."

Keeping my head down, I quickly crossed the room and followed my mom out into the hallway, feeling like I could explode at any second.

"I can't believe how rude you were!" I burst out once we were far enough away from the classroom. "Why couldn't you have just waited ten minutes?"

"So that teacher could feed you some more *ice*

cream?" my mother demanded. She was walking so fast I practically had to jog to keep up with her.

I held back a groan. "I don't get it," I persisted. "Why do you have such a problem with Ms. Kern? She's been helping me a lot with everything, and she's a great teacher."

Plus, she actually listens to me, and cares *about my life,* I thought.

I swallowed as I started to realize something . . . my mom had started getting all weird after she saw me and Ms. Kern laughing together last week. She probably knew that I was way more comfortable with Ms. Kern than I was with her. And she hated it, even though it was completely her fault.

"That's it," I almost whispered. I shook my head. "You're jealous."

She stopped walking, and her face paled, but she didn't respond.

"Ms. Kern may not be *skinny*," I continued, my voice growing loud again, "but she's nice, and funny, and *she* doesn't care at all about stuff like ice cream and calories."

My mother stared at me with wide, horrified eyes, as if I'd just slapped her. A wave of hurt and guilt washed over me, but I couldn't take back what I'd said.

I took off down the hall, tears stinging my eyes.

Anna

I should have done this a long time *ago*, I thought as I sorted through all the junk in the bottom of my closet on Monday afternoon. I couldn't believe some of the stuff I was finding in here—I wouldn't have been surprised to come across a new life-form.

I pushed aside a pile of some old scarves and the sweatshirt I practically lived in for all of sixth grade, and I noticed a book cover peeking through. I reached in and pulled the book out from the clothes. The title, which had been stamped in gold, was almost completely worn away. I traced the fading letters with my fingers—*Poopy Bear and the Magic Potty*. Below the title was a picture of Poopy Bear sitting on his magic potty, with the Potty Fairy fluttering above his head, magic wand in hand.

I opened the cover and read the inscription on the inside:

For my little sister, Anna.

Anna

I hope you learn to use the potty soon.
Then you won't stink anymore.
Love, your big brother, Tim.

I sucked in my breath, taken off guard by my brother's handwriting. Tim must have been eight or nine when he gave the book to me. I'd forgotten all about it. I flipped through the pages, smiling as I scanned the familiar illustrations. Suddenly something long, thin, and green fell out of the book. I blinked.

Tim's green braid.

I bit my lip, then picked it up. Tears gathered in my eyes as I fingered the braid, and my throat tightened up so much that it was hard to breathe.

Tim's green braid.

Why did it hurt so badly still? I swallowed, trying to fight back the sadness. After all this time, losing him was still so painful.

I instinctively reached for the phone. Salvador would know how to make this okay, how to keep me calm. He always did.

I paused with my hand on the receiver. *I can't call Salvador,* I realized. After the way he'd treated me lately, I wasn't so sure I still had a best friend.

My eyes flicked over to a note tacked onto my bulletin board with Larissa's phone number.

Maybe I don't have a best *friend,* I thought. *But I do have a friend I can call.*

I quickly dialed her number, and she picked up after a couple of rings.

"Hi. Larissa?"

"Hey, Anna! What's up?"

Wow—she sounded so happy to hear my voice.

I took a deep breath, the air finally coming in again.

Then I flopped down on my bed, still clutching Tim's braid. Now that I had her on the phone, I didn't really know what to say. I mean, I wasn't ready to tell her about the whole Tim thing. I knew she'd understand, but it felt too personal to explain to someone I still didn't know that well.

"I was just, uh, cleaning out my closet," I said.

Larissa giggled. "Yuck! Did your mum make you?"

"No," I said. "This is a case of purely self-inflicted torture," I joked, feeling my heart rate slow back down to normal. "I couldn't deal with the mess."

"Been there," Larissa said. "So how did your mum and dad like your hair?"

"Well, they didn't totally freak," I said. "But they weren't as cool about it as your parents."

Larissa laughed. "They're used to me doing crazy things," she explained. "There was this one time, though, when Bianca and I found a store that sold these freaky colored contact lenses. I bought this lime green pair and came home wearing them." She stopped, laughing harder. "My mum took one look at my eyes and just stood there in shock. You could have run her over, and she wouldn't have blinked!"

I froze, my breath catching. Larissa was just joking around—she didn't know that my brother was killed in a car accident. But I couldn't force out even a halfhearted chuckle.

"Anna? Hello?"

"Uh, y-yeah. I'm still here," I stammered.

"Are you okay? You sound really strange."

I gulped. "I'm fine, really. I just choked on some soda," I lied.

"Oh, good. I mean, I'm sorry you choked, but I'm glad it wasn't something I said."

"No, I'm fine, really," I said hastily. "But actually, I have to go. I think my mom is calling me."

"Okay. I'll see you tomorrow at school."

"Yeah. See you tomorrow," I said.

I hung up, then hugged Tim's braid against me as a few tears slid down my cheeks.

Salvador del Valle's
Top-Five Reasons Why Anna Wang
Shouldn't Have Dyed Her Hair

5. Her shocking appearance could cause major traffic accidents in town.
4. She could frighten small children and animals.
3. She could get mistaken for a Raggedy Ann doll.
2. There's absolutely nothing wrong with black hair—and there's *no reason to change things if nothing's wrong with them!*
1. She doesn't look like Anna anymore.

A n n a

I clenched my hands into fists at my sides as I headed toward Salvador's locker during break on Tuesday afternoon.

I had to have heard wrong, I told myself as I strode quickly down the hall. Those kids in the cafeteria couldn't have been talking about *Zone* when they said there was a new school Web 'zine. I mean, I know I missed a couple of meetings, and I know things have been weird between me and Salvador, but they would have told me before doing something like that. Brian or Elizabeth at least would have called me, right?

I guess I'll find out, I thought as I caught sight of Salvador, standing by his locker, stuffing books inside it. I took a deep breath, fighting back the weird nervous feeling that had suddenly come over me.

"Salvador?" I said as I came up behind him.

He spun around. "Anna," he blurted out, surprised. Then his features settled into an angry, unwelcoming frown.

"Look," I began, not quite meeting his eye, "I overheard some kids saying something about a Web site. Like, a Web 'zine or whatever," I babbled. "That's not *Zone,* right?"

Salvador snorted. "As if you care," he muttered.

My cheeks flushed. "Of course I care about *Zone.* What is that supposed to mean?"

Salvador shook his head. "Well, you certainly have a weird way of showing it," he said. "Actually, I think the word *weird* pretty much sums up the way you've been acting lately."

"What is this—some kind of revenge?" I burst out. "You don't like the fact that I have new friends, so you go ahead and make decisions about *Zone* without me?" I swallowed, unable to believe Salvador would sink this low. "You know, we're not in kindergarten anymore."

He flinched, and for a second I felt a flash of guilt. Then he reached out and slammed his locker door shut, turning back to me with hard, glaring eyes.

"In case you've forgotten," he said coldly, "I'm not the only other person on the *Zone* staff. Brian, Elizabeth, and I made the decision together to take the 'zine to the Web. And we tried waiting for you, but after you blew off three meetings, we figured we couldn't wait forever."

I gulped, glancing down at the floor. It was true—I hadn't been around lately, and I knew I'd

109

messed up. But still, they could have given me some kind of warning or something!

"This isn't really about *Zone,* is it?" Salvador continued. "It's about trading in your old friends—and your old *hair,*" he added, "for a bunch of fakes and phonies."

I held back a frustrated scream. Why did I have to *trade?*

"Sal," I said softly, "I still want to be friends with you and Elizabeth, and I still want to work on *Zone.* But I'm not going to stop hanging out with Larissa or going to drama club, so—"

"Whatever," Salvador interrupted. He shrugged. "*Zone* is doing just fine without you, and so am I."

He turned and walked away, and I slumped against his locker, feeling like someone had just knocked the wind out of me.

Kristin

"How about these?" My mom held up a pair of black denim overalls and smiled encouragingly.

"I don't think so," I replied, my eyes flicking around Fashion Train. I still didn't get why my mom had dragged me to the mall this afternoon. I guess she figured it was better to buy me new clothes than actually *talk* about the fight we'd had yesterday.

I felt really bad about our argument too. But spending the afternoon letting Mom steer me toward "flattering" clothing wasn't my idea of how to make up.

"Oh, this is perfect!" she exclaimed from the far end of the rack.

I turned to see what she was holding up and actually cringed when I caught sight of the green jumper.

"Uh, no, Mom," I said. "I don't think green is my color."

My mother frowned and studied the jumper. "I

thought the color would set off your hair," she explained. "Besides, solid colors are very flattering."

My stomach was already in knots, and it was only four o'clock. We could be here for hours.

"Hey, why don't we get something to eat?" I suggested. I had to get out of this store.

"Well, all right, dear." She frowned. "But I'm not sure there's any suitable place in the mall."

I bit my lip, visualizing the food court. I could have gone for a burrito from the Tex-Mex place, but I knew that would be out of the question.

"Oh, wait," my mom said, her face brightening. "How about The Jolly Green Bean? They've got a great spinach salad."

I was starting to have second thoughts about the snack thing. "You know, I'm not really that hungry, actually," I lied. "And we haven't looked at the sales rack yet."

Mom smiled. "Whatever you say," she agreed. We walked over to a rack marked Clearance, and I began flipping through the dresses.

My eyes landed on a midnight blue, cotton-knit tank dress.

"Mom, what about this one?" I asked her.

My mother stared at it, a disapproving crease appearing on her forehead. "I don't know, Kristin," she said.

"What's wrong with it?" I asked, holding the

dress up to my body in one of the store's nearby mirrors. "And it would match those navy platforms I just got too."

Mom wrinkled her nose. "It's too dressy for school, sweetie. And it's so . . . clingy," she blurted out.

"What's wrong with that?" I asked. I hung the dress back up, my hand starting to tremble as I realized what she meant. "I guess anyone who isn't a stick can't wear tight dresses, right?"

My mother shook her head. "Kristin, that's not what I was—"

"I know what you were saying," I cut her off. "Why do you always have to make such a big deal about my weight? Why can't you just drop it like—like other people?"

"Like Ms. Kern?" My mother stared at me, her eyes flashing.

I paused. "Yes, like Ms. Kern," I replied. Then I turned and stalked out of the store.

Zone Home Page

Hey, everyone! Welcome to the new Zone Web 'zine. We're just getting started, but soon we'll have tons of articles, reviews, and cartoons for you! Click on Reactions below to let us know what you think of the site so far, or click on Submissions if you'd like to submit something. We'll have new stuff all the time—so make sure you check us out every day!

Editors

A n n a

It looks good, I thought, staring at the *Zone* home page on my computer screen.

They hadn't posted much stuff yet, just an announcement about *Zone* going online and a couple of short articles that Elizabeth probably wrote. But the design was really cool.

I guess Brian took care of that, I thought. *He's the computer whiz.*

I'd been thinking about checking out the new *Zone* Web site ever since I came home from drama club, but it had taken me a couple of hours to actually do it. Now I wasn't sure if I should have even looked at all—it hurt to see something I used to be a part of and know that I didn't have anything to do with it anymore.

I folded my arms across my chest, squinting as I noticed a link at the bottom of the page that I'd missed before.

Anna-gram.

I moved the mouse over the word and clicked on it, waiting anxiously while the page finished loading. When the picture came on the screen, I sat back in shock.

It was a small, animated cartoon of a bat flapping one wing, like it was waving. Salvador knows that I have this weird thing for bats—I've always thought they're really cool.

I focused in on the letters printed inside a little speech balloon coming out of the bat's mouth. It was a scrambled message—an anagram. Salvador and I used to love unscrambling anagrams together. I concentrated on the words:

I sims ym steb drifen.

I blinked. *I miss my best friend?*

A smile spread across my face. After what Salvador had said to me earlier, I'd figured he really didn't want to be friends anymore. But I should have realized he was just being Salvador— saying stupid stuff out of pride.

He must have hoped I'd see this, I thought, feeling a warm glow inside. Salvador always apologizes to me in sweet, goofy ways like that—when he actually apologizes for stuff, I mean.

I jumped up and reached over to grab my phone, then stopped when I realized the phone line was tied up because I was online.

Maybe I shouldn't call anyway, I thought. Salvador had let me know that he still cared about our friendship in a really public way, on a Web site where anyone else could see it. So maybe I should do the same thing.

To: *Zone* Reactions
From: ANA3
Re: Fan E-mail

Dear Staff—
   Great job, guys. The Web site looks amazing.
   By the way, this one goes out to the very talented cartoonist:
   Em oot!
                        —Anna(gram) Wang

P.S. Are you thinking of starting a poetry corner? If so, I know someone who might be interested.

Kristin

"Hey, Kristin!"

I turned around and saw Lacey jogging down the hallway toward me, her dark hair swinging as she ran.

I sighed. It was Wednesday afternoon, and I had only a few minutes left of my break. I was on my way to see Ms. Kern, but if Lacey wanted to talk to me, I probably wouldn't get too far.

"Hey, what's up?" I asked without much enthusiasm.

She frowned. "What's the matter with you?" she asked, squinting at me. "It's not like *you* have to live with Victoria," she added, rolling her eyes.

Victoria is Lacey's stepmom, and Lacey can't stand her. Victoria *is* pretty obnoxious, but right now all I could think was how lucky Lacey was that at least Victoria wasn't her *real* mom.

"No, I just have to live with former model, Margie Seltzer," I muttered.

Lacey's expression softened, and I could tell

119

she was really worried. Lacey can be pretty self-
ish sometimes, but she does care about me.

"Did something happen with your mom?" she
asked, shifting her backpack up onto her shoulder.

I glanced past Lacey, down the hall at the
music department. "Look, I don't really want to
get into it now," I said. I looked back at Lacey
and saw the familiar expression of hurt and annoyance in her eyes that appears whenever she
feels pushed aside.

"I promise I'll fill you in later," I assured her. I
gave her a quick smile, then took off down the
hall, hoping Ms. Kern would have a minute.

Luckily she was alone in her classroom, and
she grinned when I walked in, so I guess I
wasn't bothering her.

"Hi, Kristin," she greeted me.

"Hi," I said. I sat down in a chair right in front
of her desk, trying to think of what to say next.

"Um, I'm really sorry for how my mom acted
on Monday," I blurted out. "She's . . . she just
doesn't always think about stuff like that, I
guess." I shifted uncomfortably. "I mean, about
how rude she can be to people when she doesn't
totally agree with them." I rolled my eyes. "She
freaks out when she sees me doing something
she doesn't *approve* of or whatever, like the ice
cream sundaes at the meeting."

Ms. Kern tilted her head. "It's okay," she replied. "She's just trying to watch out for you—that's how moms are. They worry about their daughters."

I glanced down at the floor, twisting my hands together in my lap. If my mom was "worried," it was probably just because she thought I'd gain a couple of extra pounds or something.

"Thanks, Ms. Kern," I said, jumping up. "I'd better get to class."

I hurried out of the room before she had a chance to respond.

I knew Ms. Kern was trying to be nice, but she just didn't understand my mom. Unfortunately, I didn't either.

A n n a

"Hello, Wang residence," I said. My voice came out a little breathless since I'd grabbed the phone on my way out the door.

"My parents would give anything for me to sound that proper when I answered the phone," a familiar voice replied.

I laughed. "Hey, Larissa. What's up?"

"Well," she said, "I was hoping you could come to the mall with me this afternoon. I just want to pick up some last-minute stuff for the skit Friday night."

I frowned. It sounded like fun, but I was heading over to surprise Salvador with one of our favorite videos. We hadn't had a chance to talk much in school today, but after the messages we'd posted on *Zone* yesterday, I figured it was the right time to try and make up.

"Sorry," I said, "but there's something I have to do."

"But I need you," Larissa whined. "I'm picking out a stud for Toby, and I'm soooo nervous about getting the right one."

122

"But Toby doesn't have any piercings," I said, confused.

"He does now," Larissa sang into the phone.

"Are you serious? Where?"

"Just his ear," Larissa said. "Nothing too interesting. And he's such a baby—he said he almost passed out from the pain."

"It's a guy thing," I said with a laugh. "If you can wait till tomorrow, I'll go with you after rehearsal," I suggested.

"Yeah, I guess tomorrow's okay," Larissa replied. "He got his hole yesterday, so it'll be a while before he can put in a new stud anyway."

"Great. See you tomorrow."

"Okay. Have fun with whatever you're doing."

"Thanks. Bye."

I hung up and grabbed my jacket, then headed out to the video store, wondering if I should have asked Larissa to wish me good luck instead.

Elizabeth

"Hello? Liz?"

I glanced across the kitchen table at my sister in confusion. "What? Did you say something?" I asked.

She sighed. "Mom, is it me, or is Liz acting like a zombie lately?" she asked.

My mom put down the carrot she'd been peeling and walked over to me and Jessica.

"You have seemed a little down," she said to me as she sat down in the chair next to mine. "Is something bothering you?"

I glanced back and forth between my mom and Jessica. Both of their gazes were fixed on my face, with matching worried expressions.

"It's Anna and Salvador," I explained. "They've been fighting nonstop lately, and I'm starting to worry about them." I shook my head, then turned to my mom. "So how do I get them to talk to each other?" I asked.

She smiled sadly. "There's not much you can do," she said. "It's up to them. But if their friendship is as strong as you always say it is, I wouldn't worry too much. They'll pull through it."

"Thanks, Mom," I said, giving her a grateful smile. I just hoped she was right.

A n n a

I reached up to ring Salvador's doorbell, noticing that my hand was trembling slightly.

Please let him be happy to see me, I thought. I tapped my foot as I waited.

Finally the door opened, and I was face-to-face with Salvador. His face paled a little in surprise.

"Anna," he said.

"Hey," I began, trying to sound casual. "So, I don't know if you've heard of this, um, mysterious new disease—it's called Jim Carrey–itis. The symptoms are unmistakable—an overwhelming urge to watch *Dumb and Dumber* for the seven-hundredth time, make dorky faces, and spend the afternoon with your best friend."

He started to smile, and my whole body relaxed in relief.

"You've got that too?" he asked. "At least we won't infect each other. It'll be like when we both had chicken pox together in the second grade."

I handed him the popcorn I'd picked up at

126

the video store, then followed him inside.

"I'll go nuke this," Salvador said, holding up the popcorn. "I'll be right back."

He disappeared into the kitchen, and I flopped down on the sofa in front of the TV. While I was flipping through channels with the remote, I heard the phone ring. Salvador picked it up in the kitchen.

"Oh, hi, Mrs. Wang," I heard him say. I immediately sat up and lowered the volume on the TV. Why was my mom calling?

"Yeah, she's in the other room. Do you want me to put her on?" Salvador asked. "Oh, okay. Sure, no problem . . . Uh-huh . . . uh-huh . . . When? . . . Uh-huh . . . uh-huh . . ."

One more "uh-huh" and I was going to scream. What could they possibly be talking about?

"Sure, no problem. Bye, Mrs. Wang." Salvador hung up. A minute later he sailed into the living room, carrying a bowl of popcorn and two cans of soda.

"Was that my mom on the phone?" I asked.

"Oh—yeah." Salvador placed the bowl on the coffee table, handed me a soda, then picked up the video. "She just wanted to make sure you got to my place okay. It, uh, took her a while to get that out, though." He walked over to the VCR and slipped in the video.

I rolled my eyes. "I knew it wouldn't last," I muttered.

"What?"

"Well, it's just that my mom has been acting more, I don't know, *normal* lately," I explained.

"That's great, Anna." Salvador plunked down beside me on the sofa.

"But if she just called to check on me, that means she's getting back into that overprotective stuff again," I said.

Salvador tossed a piece of popcorn into his mouth. "Look, Anna," he said gently, "it's great that your mom's doing better. But it still hasn't been that long. I mean, it's okay if she still worries sometimes, you know?" He smiled, and I felt a familiar sense of comfort and warmth. I hadn't realized how much I'd wanted to talk to someone about what was going on lately at home. Salvador really did know me better than anyone.

"Hey," he continued, "speaking of time, how long are you going to live with that major mistake staring back at you in the mirror?"

"What?" I asked, startled.

Salvador laughed and rolled his eyes. "You know." He tugged on my hair. "This."

I frowned. "Sal, I *like* it red," I said. "I'm not changing it back."

Salvador stared at me in disbelief. "You are kidding, right?"

I sighed. "No, Salvador, I'm not kidding. And I really don't see why it's such a big deal to you what color my hair is."

Salvador shook his head. "Next you'll be telling me you still want to hang out with Larissa and those other drama freaks."

"They're not freaks," I argued. "And why wouldn't I keep hanging out with them?" I'd thought Salvador was over all this—he'd posted that sweet message, and he'd been so happy to see me today. . . .

"I don't get it," Salvador said. "If you're still friends with them, then what was all this about?" he asked, waving his hand at the popcorn.

I glanced at Salvador's expression, noticing the deep, puzzled crease between his eyebrows. He seemed genuinely confused.

"This was about spending time with my best friend," I said. "It doesn't mean you're my *only* friend."

"I can't believe you, Anna." Salvador jumped up, stalked over to the VCR, and ejected the cassette. "Can't you see what a bunch of losers those people are?"

"If anyone's the loser, it's you!" I yelled back, starting to get really angry. "And if you're really so immature that you can't handle me having other friends besides you, then maybe we shouldn't be friends at all." I stood up and threw my jacket back on.

"Fine," Salvador shouted back. He shoved the video into its case and handed it to me. "If that's what you want, then you've got it."

I turned and rushed toward the front door, blinking back tears. I could hear Salvador screaming something about "Raggedy Ann" as I slammed the door behind me.

Algebra Class, Thursday, 9:23 A.M.

Anna,
    Salvador told me about your fight yesterday. I'm really sorry. I wish there was something I could do to get you two to make up.
                    -Elizabeth

Liz,
    Thanks, but Salvador just needs to grow up and get that I'm allowed to have other friends, even if he doesn't like them.
                                -Anna
    P.S. He might never get it.

a,
    You guys have been friends forever! There's no way you can give that up.
                    -E

Liz,
    I tried. It's up to him.
                        -A

Kristin

I let out a long sigh as I walked into my apartment after school on Thursday. My mom and I had barely spoken since our trip to the mall on Tuesday, and the last place I wanted to be was home.

Luckily she wasn't in the living room as I passed through, so I hurried into my bedroom and shut the door behind me. I dropped my backpack by my desk and then glanced over at my bed.

There was some kind of blue material draped over my pillow. *What's that?* I wondered. As I walked closer, I realized it was a dress. I picked it up and held it out in front of me.

I gasped. It was the dress I'd seen at the mall with my mom!

She must have bought it for me, I realized. I sat down on the bed, still clutching the dress. Then I lifted it up to check the size since my mom always gets me clothes that are way too small out of some kind of wishful thinking or something.

It's the right size, I thought in amazement as I

stared at the tag. Tears stung the back of my eyelids.

I jumped up and rushed into my mom's bedroom. She was lying on her bed, reading a magazine, but she glanced up when I came in. Her eyes darted back and forth between me and the dress, and she gave me a nervous smile.

I shifted from one foot to the other, not sure what to say.

"Thanks, Mom," I finally said, smiling back at her shyly. "It looks even more amazing than it did in the store."

"I bet it'll look even better on you," Mom replied.

I bit my lip, afraid I'd start to cry right there. How long had I waited for her to say something like that to me?

"Go ahead—try it on," she urged.

I hurried back to my room, threw off my shirt and jeans, and slipped on the dress. The soft fabric felt great against my skin. I turned and looked at myself in the mirror. The dress fit like it was made for me.

"I was right," my mom said from the doorway. I spun around and saw her watching me. "You look beautiful, sweetie," she said. She narrowed her eyes and peered at me closely, and I felt my body stiffen. I glanced down, trying to see if my hips were bulging or something.

"The only thing missing is sheer, navy panty hose," she announced after a moment.

I sighed, relieved.

"I've only got sheer black," I said.

"So why don't we stop by the mall tomorrow night?" she suggested. "We can pick up some panty hose, and . . ." She trailed off, a strange, wistful expression in her eyes.

"Are you sure?" I asked.

She nodded. "Unless you have plans," she added, frowning slightly.

I winced. The athletes' brunch that Bethel had been working on was this morning, so she and I were going to have a big meeting with all the carnival committee volunteers tomorrow after school. I really wanted to be there, since Bethel hadn't been involved until now.

"I, uh, I did have something . . . ," I began. My mom glanced away, but not before I saw a glimmer of disappointment in her eyes. "But it's nothing important," I added quickly. "I mean, I can just postpone it. I'd rather go to the mall with you anyway."

"Really?" She looked back at me, her face brightening.

"Yeah, really," I said softly. And the amazing thing was that I actually meant it.

Anna

I pulled the curtain slightly aside and peeked through the opening at the audience.

Where are they? I wondered. It was Friday night, and any minute now the lights would dim and we'd be onstage, performing our skit for the drama-club parents' night. There was just one problem—my parents weren't there.

Maybe Dad's having trouble finding a parking space, I thought. I could maybe believe that if I hadn't just seen tons of empty spots in front of the school when I was outside a little while ago.

I'd actually been pretty surprised when my parents had said they'd come tonight. Even though they've both been acting so much more normal lately, coming out in public like this was a *huge* step for my mom. I'd even been almost okay with the idea that my parents wouldn't be in the audience.

But they'd seemed *excited* to come see me, so I'd gotten excited too. And now if they didn't show up, I wasn't sure how I'd get through the night.

"Hey, are you all right?" Larissa asked, coming up behind me.

I spun around, forcing a smile. "Yeah, I'm fine—just butterflies," I half lied. If Salvador was there, he'd understand—he'd know exactly what I was really worried about. But now wasn't the time to fill Larissa in on the past year of my life or my crazy family.

"At least you just have butterflies," Larissa said. "I think there's a herd of wild bees thundering around in my stomach."

I laughed.

"I like this feeling, though," Larissa added. "It's such a rush, you know?"

"Yeah," I acknowledged. "It is." I'd never thought I would *enjoy* this sensation—my whole body jumping with nervousness. But Larissa was right—the adrenaline made me feel so *alive*.

I'd be fine if I knew my parents were out there, I thought, staring at the curtain again. I'd let it close when Larissa startled me, so I couldn't see the audience anymore.

"Come on," Larissa said, grabbing my arm, "let's get back into the studio."

I followed her into the room backstage where the rest of the members of the drama club were getting ready.

Studying my face in the mirror, I couldn't

help but scrunch up my nose in disgust. Stage makeup is much heavier than the normal stuff—Larissa had explained that it's so your features can stand out more to the audience.

"Okay, everyone," Mr. Dowd announced from the other side of the room. "We're on in five. Is everyone pumped?"

We all cheered, and I felt a wave of happiness. It was so great to really be a *part* of something—the energy in the room was amazing.

I quickly touched up my lipstick and ran a brush through my hair, then glanced down at my costume to make sure everything was in place. It was actually pretty ironic—for my role I had to wear a pink terry-cloth bathrobe and fuzzy, pink slippers. It was practically my mom's uniform for almost the whole year after Tim died.

Larissa draped her arm around me and grinned. "You look perfect," she said. "Frumpy, like a dumped girlfriend. How about me?" She spun around in her tight black pants and shirt.

"You make a great cat burglar," I replied.

Mr. Dowd strode over to us. "Ladies, assume your places onstage. One minute to curtain time."

Larissa and I gave each other a good-luck hug and hurried onstage. Toby was already in position. Even in the semidarkness I could see the nervousness in his face.

Anna

"Are you all right?" I whispered to him.

"If you call sweaty palms, nausea, and dizziness all right, I'm doing great," he answered.

Larissa and I exchanged worried glances. "Toby, you'll be fine," Larissa encouraged. She gave his arm a reassuring squeeze.

"Yeah. Don't worry. We're right here with you," I added.

"Thanks, guys." He swallowed hard. "I just hope I don't blow my lines."

Mr. Dowd gave the cue, and the curtain slowly rose. A hush fell over the audience as the house lights dimmed. Suddenly the stage was bathed in light. I glanced at the audience out of the corner of my eye, but I couldn't see past the first two rows.

I took a deep breath. "Marvin! What are you doing here?" I said loudly. The steadiness of my voice helped to calm my jitters. I hoped it would have that effect on Toby too.

The rest of the performance was a magical blur. I lost myself completely in my character, just like I had in rehearsals. It was like Anna ceased to exist onstage and "Susan" took over. I guess Larissa and Toby got caught up in the excitement too. Toby didn't flub his lines once, and Larissa was everything a cool lady cat burglar should be. And when my big moment arrived, the tears flowed effortlessly. I didn't even have to drag up any hurt feelings from the past. It was as if Susan's pain was my pain. I guess the audience must have felt it too. People were sniffling and blowing their noses all over the theater by the time I said my last line.

When it was over, we held our places onstage as the lights dimmed. My heart raced in anticipation of the audience's reaction. Would they clap politely because it was expected of them? Or would they applaud like they really meant it? I had my answer a second later when a wave of thunderous applause washed over the theater.

I sucked in my breath in amazement—the sound was actually almost deafening. Larissa, Toby, and I joined hands and faced the audience. As we took a collective bow, I could see people starting to rise to their feet. We were getting a standing ovation—every actor's dream!

Larissa squeezed my hand. "Great job, Anna!" She shouted over the applause.

I smiled at her and turned to Toby. His cheeks were flushed with excitement. He caught my eye and mouthed the word, "Thanks."

I turned back to the audience as the house lights started to come back up, my eyes flicking across the parents and kids. Suddenly my breath caught, and my heart started to race all at once.

My parents were there, standing in front of

their seats right in the center section, a few rows back from the stage. I stared at them, stunned and thrilled, and then glanced next to my dad. Elizabeth stood next to him, and on the other side of her was . . .

Salvador.

I nearly stumbled backward when I caught sight of him.

My gaze swept across the four of them, and my eyes filled with tears as I saw the pride beaming out of their faces.

All of their faces—including Salvador's.

Kristin

"Is that all you need? Just the panty hose?" my mom asked as we left Fashion Train on Friday night.

"I think I'm all set," I said. "Thanks, Mom, I can't wait to wear these with the dress."

My mom smiled. "I can't wait to see you in the whole outfit," she said. "I bet Brian will like it too," she added, her eyes twinkling.

My eyebrows shot up. That was a first—my mom never mentions Brian. Sometimes I wonder if she even realizes we're together, even though of course I told her when he asked me to be his girlfriend.

Either aliens had abducted my mother and left this new mom in her place, or the stuff I'd said had actually made her hear me for the first time in my life.

We passed by the card store as we walked down the mall, and I noticed a pretty little merry-go-round figurine in the display window.

I paused, thinking about how nice Ms. Kern

had been today when I'd explained that I had to postpone the big meeting with Bethel until next week. I'd wanted to get her something to say thanks for all the help she'd given me with the carnival planning and also just for being so nice. I craned my neck, trying to see the price tag.

"See something you like?" my mother asked.

I bit my lip, wondering what she'd do if I admitted that I wanted to get Ms. Kern a present. Things had been going so well between us—I wasn't up for another fight. But I really wanted to do this.

I took a deep breath. "Well," I began, "I thought it might be nice to show Ms. Kern how much I appreciate all the work she's doing on the carnival."

I clenched my teeth as I waited for my mother's response. Her expression darkened for a second but then relaxed back into a smile.

"I think that's a good idea, Kristin," she said. "Giving her a little gift would be a really sweet gesture."

I studied my mother's expression for some sign of hidden anger, but her smile seemed sincere.

"Come on," she said, taking my arm and gently guiding me into the card store. "Show me what you have in mind."

We walked in, and I pointed out the merry-go-round.

"It sort of has a carnival theme," I explained.

"Even though I know we won't be able to have merry-go-rounds at school or anything," I added with a laugh.

"It's only ten dollars," my mom said, examining the price tag. "Why don't we get it?"

I grinned. "Great," I said. We found one in a box on a nearby shelf, grabbed it, and then went to wait in line at the counter.

I glanced outside the store while we waited, noticing the entrance to I Scream a few stores down on the other side of the mall. Just the bright, neon ice cream cone over the sign was enough to make my mouth water.

"Um, Mom, would it be okay if we stopped for some ice cream before we leave?" I asked her. Usually I'd never even bother asking, but after the way she'd been acting tonight . . .

My mother's eyes narrowed, and her facial muscles tensed. "I don't think that's such a good idea, Kristin," she said in the sharp, disapproving tone I recognized. It was her junk-food–red-alert! voice. "After all, you haven't had dinner yet."

I held back a smile.

At least I know she wasn't possessed by aliens, I thought. The words *ice cream* still inspired utter terror in her.

She was the same old Margie Seltzer. But maybe that wasn't such a bad thing after all.

A n n a

"Anna, you're a star!" Mr. Dowd exclaimed from behind me as I finished slathering on a layer of cold cream. "You and Larissa and Toby were dynamite out there. I can't believe this was your first time performing in front of a crowd—you're a pro!"

The skits were all over, and the entire club was in the studio backstage, taking off our makeup and changing out of our costumes.

"Thanks," I said shyly, wiping off my face with a wad of Kleenex. "I'm really glad you think so."

Mr. Dowd stared at me in surprise. "It's not just me, Anna," he replied, shaking his head. "Did you hear the applause? Not every actor gets a standing ovation her first time onstage. Just ask your excellent costars."

Larissa and Toby had finished changing out of their costumes and were heading toward us. Toby gave a little tug on my ponytail when he and Larissa reached us.

"Thanks for saving my butt out there, Anna," he said, grinning at me.

I cocked my head in confusion. "What did I do?"

"I almost freaked when the curtain went up," Toby explained. He shrugged. "I don't know what my problem was—usually I'm fine. But tonight I was a real mess. Then I heard your voice, and you sounded so sure of yourself. I guess your confidence was contagious." His smile broadened. "Anyway, you really helped."

"Yeah. You were *awesome,* Anna," Larissa added, giving me a quick hug.

"That's coming from one of the brightest actresses I've ever worked with," Mr. Dowd put in. Larissa beamed at the compliment. "So you should be proud," he finished.

I flushed. I was proud—*extremely* proud. But I was also dying to see my parents and Elizabeth and Salvador. This was such a huge moment for me, and even though Toby and Larissa were great, I wanted to share it with the people who knew me best.

"Uh-oh, we're being invaded," Toby said, nodding up at the doorway at the top of the stairs. Parents and other SVJH students were crowding into the room and filing down the steps. "This always happens after shows," he explained to me. "Oh, there's my dad—I'll see you

145

guys later." He rushed off to find his father.

I glanced up at all the people, searching for familiar faces. Then I lowered my gaze to the ones who were already wandering around the room, and suddenly I saw my parents coming right toward me. Mom was carrying a bouquet of flowers.

"You were wonderful, honey!" she said as she thrust the flowers into my hands. I stared at her in shock. Her whole face was lit up with happiness, an emotion that I hadn't connected with her in so long, it almost seemed impossible.

"Thanks," I whispered, clutching the flowers as I blinked away tears.

Dad stepped forward and kissed me on the cheek. "Great job, sweetie," he said.

"Thanks, Dad," I said. "By the way, Mom, Dad, this is Larissa."

"I figured," my father said, smiling as he pointed up at her hair.

Larissa giggled. "Did Anna tell you the color was my idea, Mr. Wang?" she asked.

"Well," my father mused, "your name did come up. But Anna has always had her own mind. No one can talk her into anything she doesn't want to do."

"In other words," I interjected, "you're off the hook."

We all laughed again, and then I caught sight

of Elizabeth and Salvador, walking toward us.

Elizabeth gave me a hug as soon as she reached me. "Anna, you were amazing," she whispered in my ear.

"Thanks," I said, starting to feel overwhelmed from all the praise. I glanced at Salvador, then looked back at Elizabeth, raising my eyebrows questioningly. She shrugged.

"Hey, I have to run," Larissa said. "Nice to meet you both," she said to my parents.

"Nice to meet you," my dad told her.

Larissa hurried off, and I took a deep breath, wondering when Salvador was going to say anything.

"Um, we actually have to get going too," Elizabeth said, exchanging glances with my parents.

I frowned in confusion. I'd assumed my parents would give me a ride home. "But—"

"Bye," Elizabeth blurted out. Then she, my mother, and my father spun around and walked off quickly in the other direction.

I stared after them for a second, then remembered that Salvador was still standing a couple of feet away from me.

I glanced over at him, and he was watching me with a nervous, sweet smile.

"Um, you were—you were really great," he said, stuffing his hands in his pockets. "I mean—well, you're a really good actress."

"Thanks," I said. "I'm kind of surprised you came," I admitted. "After what happened Wednesday . . ."

Salvador sighed. "Yeah. Well, I recently came down with this mysterious new disease," he said. He took his hand out of his pocket and ran it through his hair, causing a couple of strands to stick straight up. I tried not to giggle.

"It strikes mostly overpossessive dorks," he continued. "It's called, uh, foot-in-the-mouth disease. The major symptom is an uncontrollable urge to make a complete fool of yourself by trying to tear down your best friend because you think she might be getting bored with you." Salvador looked down at the floor again and shifted from foot to foot. "Ever heard of it?" he asked.

I smiled. "I think so," I replied. "Hey, is there a treatment for this disease?"

Salvador finally raised his eyes up to meet mine. "I'm told if the best friend can forgive and forget, there's close to a hundred-percent recovery rate."

I giggled, then put my flowers down on the table next to me and reached out to slip my hand into Salvador's. "Consider yourself cured," I said with a smile.

"Thanks, Anna," he said. He squeezed my hand, and suddenly I knew that everything was exactly the way it should be again.

"Hey," he continued, his eyes sparkling, "are you in the mood to party?"

I laughed. "What do you mean?" I asked.

Salvador let go of my hand, then draped his arm around my shoulders and started to lead me toward the backstage exit.

"Well," he began, "I happen to know there's a big blowout over at the Wang residence, courtesy of Mr. and Mrs. Wang."

"What?" My head jerked back in surprise. "My parents are throwing me a *party?*"

So that was why they'd been in such a rush to get out of here with Elizabeth!

"Yep," Salvador replied. "Remember when your mom called me the other day, when you were over? She asked me to take care of the guest list." He paused, his cheeks turning slightly pink. "I have to admit, I kind of almost called her back Wednesday night and said I couldn't do it," he said. "You know, after you left."

We got to the door, and Salvador held it open for me, then followed me outside.

"But I realized what a jerk I was being," he said as we started to walk together along the sidewalk. "Plus Elizabeth kind of gave me a hard time," he admitted. "She told me some stuff about her and Jessica, how they both know deep down that no matter what happens or who their other friends are, they're still best friends." He stopped. "That's how it is for us, Anna, even if we're not twins or whatever. We're just always going to be best friends."

I started to smile. It was the sweetest thing he'd ever said to me.

"So I went ahead and let everyone know about the party," he said, "*including* the entire drama club. They're all coming."

I stared up at him, grinning. "Really?" I asked. "You're okay with that?"

He shrugged. "Just remember to thank me someday when you're getting your first big award," he said. He stopped walking and struck a pose like he was giving some big, important speech. "This is for my very best friend," he said in a high-pitched voice that I guess was supposed to sound like me. "Salvador del Valle. If it hadn't been for him—"

"I never would have learned how to make a fool out of myself in front of people," I interrupted, laughing.

He glared at me for a second, pretending to be offended. Then he started to laugh too, and he gave my shoulder a playful shove.

"Let's go," I said, smiling. "I can't miss my own party."

After all, I had a lot to celebrate.

Win a **SHARP**® MiniDisc Player

I. HOW TO ENTER

NO PURCHASE NECESSARY. Enter by printing your name, address, phone number, date of birth, and a name for the Web site, and mail to: SHARP & SWEET VALLEY JUNIOR HIGH MINI-DISC CONTEST, Random House Children's Books Marketing Department, 1540 Broadway, 19th Floor, New York, NY 10036. Entries must be received by Random House no later than July 15, 2000. LIMIT ONE ENTRY PER PERSON. Random House will not be able to return your submission, so please keep a copy for your records.

II. ELIGIBILITY

Contest is open to residents of the United States, excluding the state of Arizona, who are between the ages of 7 and 14 as of January 1, 2000. All federal, state, and local regulations apply. Void wherever prohibited or restricted by law. Employees of Random House, Inc., Sharp, their parents, subsidiaries, and affiliates, and employees' immediate families and persons living in their household are not eligible to enter this contest. Random House is not responsible for lost, stolen, illegible, incomplete, postage due, or misdirected entries.

III. PRIZE

One grand prize winner and five runners-up will win a Sharp MiniDisc player (approximate retail value $199.00 US).

IV. WINNER

One grand prize winner and five runners-up will be chosen on or about August 1, 2000, from all eligible entries received within the entry deadline by the Random House Children's Books Marketing Department. The contest will be judged by the Random House Children's Books Marketing Department and prizes will be awarded on the basis of creativity. The grand prize winner will win a Sharp MiniDisc player and the winning Web site name may appear in upcoming editions of Sweet Valley Junior High. The five runners-up will receive Sharp MiniDisc players. Only the winners will be notified. The prizes will be awarded in the name of the winner's parent or legal guardian. Winners will be notified by mail on or about August 15, 2000. Taxes, if any, are the winners' sole responsibility. The winner's parent or legal guardian will be required to execute and return affidavits of eligibility and release within 14 days of notification. A noncompliance within that time period or the return of any notification as undeliverable will result in disqualification and the selection of an alternate winner. In the event of any other noncompliance with rules and conditions, prize may be awarded to an alternate winner.

V. RESERVATIONS

By entering the contest you consent to the use of your name, likeness, and biographical data for publicity and promotional purposes on behalf of Random House and Sharp with no additional compensation or further permission (except where prohibited by law). Other entry names will NOT be used for subsequent mail solicitation. For the names of the winners, available after September 1, 2000, please send a stamped, self-addressed envelope to: Random House, Sharp MiniDisc Winners, 1540 Broadway, 19th Floor, New York, NY 10036.